MILLENNIAL

Hope

FREDA EMMONS

Millennial Hope
Second book in the Hope Series

Cover Design by Bethany Stroup

Published in the United States of America

ISBN-10: **1548771570**
ISBN-13: **978-1548771577**

"If you've ever wondered what the Great White Throne Judgement will be like, you'll find this book is a vision of what we look forward to one day. Freda does a great job placing us in the middle of it all. Praise God!"

LaVorna Tester

"A gift of what it could be like to live with Jesus – a beautiful vision from a lovely and inspired imagination. I believe that if everyone could dream like this, we would all be a lot more excited about being Christians!"

Kyle Sims

Dedication

For my husband, Rodney,
who has loved me so unwaveringly
and taught me to laugh,
even at myself!

Contents

List of Characters

Jesus

Sarah

Paul, Sarah's pre-Resurrection husband

Sally, Sarah's friend

Rob, Sally's pre-Resurrection husband

Ted, Rob and Sally's son

Ron, Rob and Sally's son

Bill, Rob and Sally's son

Anna, Rob and Sally's daughter

George, **Muriel**, **Sandy**, **Bridget**, **Kevin**, **Maria**, people in the first class that Sarah & Sally helped with

Eve, first of womanhood

Hannah, Samuel's mother

Leroy, Sarah's brother

Delphina, former missionary to the people of China, persecuted for her faith

Elizabeth, Sarah's sister

Sweeny, Sarah's friend from before Resurrection Morning

Jess, **Elmo**, **Samantha**, and **Amber**, some of the lost children who were found and saved by Jesus

Ben, the first lost child to receive Jesus

Jacob, the leader of the children who were found and saved.

Lester, Sarah's younger brother

Ty, Sarah's younger brother

Randy, Sarah's youngest brother

Miriam, little girl who was named after Moses' sister

Angelity

Achimeirel – meaning "constructed by God"

Abdiel – meaning "Servant of God"

Katurael – meaning "Fragrance for God"

Chapter 1
Assignment: Encourager

Sarah savored the heat of the sun, as it peeked in the window and warmed her head and shoulders. She leaned her head back and closed her eyes, contemplating all the glorious things that had happened in such a short time since arriving back on Earth. The last six months seemed to emerge from her thoughts into a vision; the people of God living in the utopia of Jesus' millennial reign on Earth. It morphed into what looked like a ribbon of hope, beauty, healing and cleansing, twisting itself into a bow and then changing colors. The ribbon then developed into a bouquet of roses, with the sweet rose fragrance filling the room with a profound awareness of the Presence of Jesus. In addition, the tender rose florets reminded her of the fellowship with Him and all the forever friends that she had come to know and cherish. Just as she opened her eyes and smiled at how the ribbon transformed into the bouquet of blessing, she noticed that she had a visitor coming up the steps of her Earth Dwelling, as she called it tenderly.

Sarah hurried, a beauty in her soft blue, lounging outfit and comfy shoes, from her favorite spot in the sun room, to the living room and opened the door even before her guest had knocked. Oh, how wonderful; it was Jesus with a gift in His arms. It was so like her Lord; He carried a magnificent vase with a large bouquet of flowers that had been crafted out of ribbon, exactly as she had seen in her vision! All the colors of the rainbow, and even more, were included. The flowers held in their folds of ribbon tender scents. Sarah could not keep from her lips a huge, "Ahhhhh." Rather than trying to carry the huge bouquet, she merely opened the door wide and motioned Jesus to come in. She stopped a moment to decide where she

1

wanted the beautiful adornment and decided on a table that she had just placed in the living room the day before and did not have anything on it. It was a high, round, ornately carved wood table and the bouquet was the perfect decoration for it. Jesus placed the bouquet in the middle of the table and they both stepped back to enjoy it; she then flung her arms open and hugged Him with all the exuberance of a little child.

Sarah exclaimed, "Thank you, Jesus! I am blessed over and over by your grace and love. This bouquet confirms to me what the Spirit was sharing with me; each ribbon began as an adjustment to our life back on Earth and changed into florets as Divine blessing filled out the details of our new lives. I love that I don't have to struggle against selfish feelings and thoughts anymore, even after our return. A lot of things have changed and we've all made modifications in how we live here. This gorgeous bouquet really blesses my heart. Thank you, my Lord, so much! Please relax here on this lounger. Would you like something to drink?"

Jesus graciously turned down the beverage, but affirmed her appraisal of His gift, as they both sat down, "No, but thanks for offering it to me. I'm glad you like the bouquet; I agree, there have been changes from living in Heaven. I love the things of Earth; the absolute beauty is my gift of honor to Father God and to our Spirit. I love creating and interacting with all that I've created. I have come with a question to ask of you. Will you assist me in our new ministry, which is beginning tomorrow morning, to those who are young in the faith? I will be teaching of my eternal truth; I would like for you to help affirm those truths with activities and offer your generous and compassionate mentoring, if you are willing?"

Sarah answered, "Oh Yes, my Lord Jesus, it would be my pleasure. How can I help?"

Jesus launched into His purpose, "I will be teaching the eternal truths of my love, provision, and grace. I am calling individuals who have the gift of encouragement to partner with me by providing engaging activities which affirm those truths. My Spirit will be with you, as you listen to the eternal truth of which I speak, infusing within your heart and mind, the details of the activity which will bless my people. Some activities will be those which you are familiar with, which you have led before, and have marveled how people have been blessed; others will be new to you, but my Spirit will guide you in every aspect. I love blessing my people and seeing their joy, as they explore new and profound ways to experience my love and grace. Life lessons which have become a part of your life of faith, can be a source of encouragement to those who are just getting their feet wet, so to speak, in their faith walk.

Hefty gatherings of young Christians are emigrating from all over the Earth, concealed pockets of believers that the anti-christ did not know about. They received me after the rapture that you experienced and therefore, they lived through the tribulation and suffered physically and emotionally during those horrible years. I adore them and want the very best for them; I am constantly available to help my beloved develop in faith and spiritual strength. My purpose is to help each individual grow spiritually and in the gifting that I have placed in them, for the uplifting of all of my family. I am confident of your ability to be a mentor and an encourager. You are uniquely gifted; I am pleased with your gentle willingness to live-out the gifting I placed in you."

Sarah replied, "I am honored that you would ask me. With You and Your Spirit ever guiding me, I will endeavor to inspire new believers."

"Excellent!" exclaimed Jesus. "I will begin with the steps which are reflected in the bouquet of ribbon, first – adjustment (learning the foundation of faith), then forming florets of faith, (the fruit of the Spirit), and finally, development and growth of those florets into lusciously fragrant bouquets of spiritual wisdom and boldness.

"Wow!" Sarah exclaimed. "I knew the Spirit had given me the vision, when I saw you bringing me the ribbon-flower bouquet. But I didn't perceive the profound correlation to our life of faith until just now, when you tied it all together. Thank you, for the vision, the bouquet and the great object lesson! I love you so, Jesus!" She reached out to give Him a hug.

Jesus received her embrace and confirmed His love for her, "I have loved you from before I created anything. You are my precious Little One. Thank you for your faithful service to God; we adore you and will provide insight and humor, as you assist our dear ones in their faith-walk."

Jesus rose and lifted his hostess up; He held her again and she flushed in the joy of that moment. As He released her, Jesus said once more, looking deep into her eyes, "I love you, Little One, my dear Sarah."

"And I love you, more than I can put into words," replied Sarah. With that, they walked slowly to the door, as though cherishing the moment. Sarah opened the door and Jesus stepped out into the warmth of the Mediterranean sun.

Closing the door gently, the delight of partnering with her Lord to encourage others in faith enveloped Sarah like hummingbirds flocking around a mass of vivacious honeysuckle vines. She meandered through her small domicile and went about her simple tasks of cleaning and having a bite to eat. As she did so, her mind was whirling with ideas of the many activities that had been a huge blessing over the years; walking in faith with her Lord was the core of her entire life. The more she allowed her thoughts to germinate, the more excited she became. She paused for prayer, stopping in the middle of straightening up her kitchen, pulled a pillow off the couch, and knelt, committing her thoughts, words, and actions to God's ultimate direction and authority.

Sarah began by breathing in and out His wonderful Name, "Abba", as she pulled air deeply into her lungs, and "Father" as she breathed out. She continued, immersed in the intense love of God, which always flooded her body with robust power whenever she prayed, imparted to her by the Spirit. "I thank you, my God, that you have chosen me to partner with you, to encourage my brothers and sisters in activities which affirm your eternal truths. I need you in every way, in order for me to be an encourager and mentor. Help me to be sensitive to your guidance and sensitive to your people. My longing is not for me to be lifted up before them, but You, Lord. Create in me a squeaky-clean heart, so that I will bring you honor and glory before those young in faith. Lord God, help me to listen empathetically and encourage insightfully. Be with me in all the details, for your Glory. In the mighty Name of Jesus, Amen."

As she paused after her prayer, Sarah felt the gentle whispering in her mind, the Spirit's response. "You do bring glory to God. Your genuineness, gentleness, compassion for people, and willing spirit are the specific reasons We entrust you with this task. We bless you, Sarah, in our abundant love."

For a long moment, Sarah just rested in that great love. It was so complete, so powerful and so desirous that she absolutely absorbed it into her soul. When she felt so satiated in the love of God that she thought her cells might explode, she slowly stood and turned to gaze upon the gorgeous ribbon floral bouquet and marveled how blessed she was.

Presently, Sarah thought about taking a walk, both physically and mentally, toward the Valley of Megiddo, back to the day of their arrival back on Earth. The Spirit quietly affirmed in her spirit that this would be a walk of reflection on the recent past, as well as a walk of experiencing the never-ending newness and brilliance of His love.

Chapter 2
A Contemplative Trek

Sarah strolled the cobblestone streets of the Jerusalem environs, soaking in the beauty, peace, and joy of life that effervesced because the Lord of the universe lived with His people. Gone were the petty arguments between neighbors, the taverns that were in reality, seedy dives of aberrant souls twisting under the behest of Satan, and the horrendous violence that oppressed victims and perpetrators. Sarah breathed in deep of the love and grace of the Lord Jesus. That love permeated everything, cleaning all of the pollution out of the air, water, and land, and replaced the awful stench of evil with a life-giving, refreshing fragrance that she reveled in.

Sarah pondered as she moseyed along what used to be an awful long hike toward the Megiddo Valley, "*How wonderful that I do not have to prepare for hours for each activity! I love living in the Presence of the King of kings! Life is easy, not a lazy easy, like I used to live before my transformation at the rapture, but an everything-is-possible easy; it is profound and simple all at the same time!*"

Her first 60+ years were often filled with anger, pain and so many other effects of a sinful world. The first life experience on Earth was replete with stupid, awful things that she did and immediately regretted. Even after committing her life to Christ, she still had a sinful nature which, thanks be to God, didn't rule over her, but still occasionally reared its ugly head and made her miserable when it did. She remembered longing for divine intervention; she had despised the petty things that were a sore spot in her spirit. She was so very thankful for Jesus' forgiveness; He endured the penalty for her every sin and reconciled her with the Triune God. Yet still, before Resurrection Morning, sin was as much a part of life on Earth as her daily need for food and water.

Then, the majesty of Christ invaded the mundane and changed everything about her life. The mortal, physical body she had held in contempt (because she had endured innumerable physical and sexual assaults to her body throughout her youth) was changed in an instant to be immortal, with no pain, nor aging. In that split second, the sin nature was sent packing from her body, spirit, and soul. She felt as if she had bathed with the best soap, which cleaned up all the pockets of grime inside and out. As she pondered, the thought came to Sarah, *I have indeed bathed, in the shed blood of Jesus, the first-fruits of the resurrection.*

She sat down for a moment, on a bench that was flanked by almost-invisible vines connecting dainty lavendar flowers and surrounded on three sides by a large grove of olive trees. The blossoms of the olive trees splashed delicate white against the dark leaves; their sweet fragrances mingled in the light breeze. Thoughts poured through Sarah's mind, flashing here and there in a whirlwind of activity. She thought about living in Heaven, how beautiful and profound life is there. The flowers are way beyond beautiful; their color, beauty and deep fragrance had captivated her. God is the source of light; there was a quality about it that was difficult to describe. Love reverberated in the light, pulsating in power and filling everyone and everything with its power. There's no sin in Heaven; it is so much easier to live the way she really wanted to, giving honor and glory to God and living in sweet fellowship with her brothers and sisters in Christ. She mused, *"Oh, that life of joy unspeakable, is here too, with Jesus as the best bonus of all!"*

The Spirit brought to her mind and heart how even before Resurrection Morning, she had been blessed greatly and had blessed others as well. In a rapid sequence, Sarah reviewed memories of how God had blessed activities which Sarah had been a part of, before the rapture. She recalled the tender tears of people receiving God's love. The Spirit affirmed those same activities would now bless even more, similar to the blooming of Earth's produce and beauty, with the Presence of the Lord Jesus Christ permeating His blessing into every plant. Sarah felt treasured, as she anticipated her new role in the lives of new disciples.

A gaggle of little children, lightheartedly giggling and chasing each other around the trees, swiftly brought her focus back to the present. Her eyes followed the cavorting children as they pursued each other through the olive grove. Refreshed by their youthful abandon, Sarah meandered in her mind once again. She recognized that even though Earth was still under the curse that began with Adam and Eve, there was a rejuvenation of life here because of the Presence of Jesus. All of the believers who experienced the rapture already had immortal bodies and had been cleansed from sin. It was so much easier to live without the pesky tendrils of sin pursuing her. However, those who had received Jesus as their Savior and Lord after the rapture, in the season of time described as the tribulation and had not been killed and joined those in Heaven, their bodies were in a transition period. Individuals experienced the changing of their bodies, from the mortal to the immortal, differently. Some described an instantaneous shift, a tangible disentangling of the sin connection with their bodies, such as infirmities lifting and physical elimination eradicating! Others describe noticing an easygoing progression, from feeling negative physically, mentally, and even emotionally, to a thrillingly optimistic feeling within their body, mind, and emotions. Sarah didn't really understand all of the changes; she wondered, "*Do the married couples still share intimacy and could they have children, or were their entire relationships transformed into the deeper relationships of brother and sister – without the physical intimacy, as hers and Paul's had been?*"

With a chuckle in His voice, The Spirit, whispered gently in her ear, "So inquisitive, my dear! It is sweet that you wonder about details. It is such an endearing aspect of your character, which I placed deep within your soul, for you see, I am totally into details and you have been made in My image. To answer your query about the Tribulation Saints, yes, there are many changes that they experience the same as you have, the purging of pain, sadness and sin from their lives. However, my eternal purpose for my people will be carried forth with this new generation, for they and their children, for as many generations as will occur during the Millennial Reign of Jesus Christ, will raise up new generations of children of the King. Therefore, Tribulation Saints will continue in marital intimacy. (Just as a side note, such intimacy is highly blessed within the marriage relationship of man and woman; it foreshadows the most intimate relationship of all, between God and His people.)"

Sarah sighed a huge "Ah," as she sent a mental "*Thank you!*" to Her Lord. She pondered for a moment how wonderful it was to converse with Her Lord any time she had an inkling to. She remembered having similar conversations with The Spirit before Resurrection Day, but now, their communication was much more vibrant and personal. She remembered how back then, everything seemed to hinge on her willingness to lean into her faith in the Lord Jesus Christ. Now, she actually experienced His Presence, both in person and in His Spirit. She giggled to herself; the fact was that she also experienced Father God and His love, just as present and powerful as was Jesus and the Spirit. They were each unique in the expression of love to her and interaction with her, yet they were one - united in every way! It was enough to make her head buzz, even though she had this new, perfected body! With a startled realization, Sarah acknowledged that the totality and utter immensity of Father God, Jesus the Savior, and The Spirit of the Living God being uniquely individual and yet one in unity, power, and love was far beyond her level of understanding. Sitting on that bench, Sarah closed her eyes and worshipped, quietly and pensively, thanking her God for all the joy of life in His Presence.

Sarah felt the affirmation of the Spirit like a whirlwind of peace that moved outward from somewhere deep within her body. She heard His gentle voice, "We love your sweet spirit. You have been given the exact abilities that are needed for assisting Jesus – you have a nurturing personality; people naturally come to you, seeking comfort, information, support and guidance. You are kind, compassionate and have a wisdom that the Father has given to you because you live so completely dedicated to God."

"Thank you so much, my God," Sarah spoke quietly. When she opened her eyes, she once again felt a peace wash over her. She never tired of receiving such a blessing; it delighted her in every molecule of her body. She rested a bit more, taking in the splendor of the nearby mountains, as well as the delightful charm of frolicking children.

A lot had happened in the short time since they arrived back on Earth. Sarah pensively thought back that eventful day, just about six months previous. Sarah, and for that matter, all of the saints that came with Jesus on the beautiful white horses, were shocked by the horrific reality of the battle of Armageddon. It was no battle at all; Jesus simply asserted, both verbally and physically, His power over all of life. The hoard of defiant populace refused to acknowledge that is was by the power of Jesus that they were even breathing. Jesus simply removed that grace upon their lives and they fell dead immediately. They did not suffer, nor did they thrash about. Their bodies simply stopped functioning and they dropped like 100 lb. bricks. Then, the birds came and gorged on their bodies. It was appalling. The throng of believers had not stayed long, but turned from the carnage, as Jesus led them from the place of death.

Sarah had not been back to the Valley of Megiddo since that day, but she found herself drawn to go there now, to see what had become of the mass of bodies that littered the ground. As she stood to resume the hike out to the Valley of Megiddo, a warm breeze blew her long wavy locks of hair all over. She laughed and simply caught it up into a loose braid and bound it with a ribbon-laden elastic band she always carried in her pocket. As she did so, she mused about how much she herself had changed since that long ago Resurrection Morning. The most remarkable change was the lack of pain in her body. Having her health restored and her body rejuvenated by the power of her Lord had been absolutely delightful! But there were more changes that brought her blessing upon blessing. Sarah remembered how, before Resurrection Morning, her hair was thin and greying; the subtle signs of aging were not so subtle at all! After Resurrection Morning, her hair had thickened into luxurious tresses that waved and curled, just as she had always longed for. Gone was the fat that she had put on so easy and struggled endlessly to get rid of. She didn't even have left-over skin hanging around! Most significantly of all, she no longer had ongoing issues of self-loathing, which she had previously struggled to overcome. Jesus, the miracle designer, transformed her life so completely that she deeply loved herself and therefore, was able to love others profoundly. She no longer tinkered with the temptations of being judgmental, gossiping, and having a sweeping anger that used to flare up at the slightest provocation. The Lord renovated her emotions to be the very best part of her personality, the person she was created to be! Now, her life oozed with empathy, tenderness, sweetness, confidence and a love so profound that words were not enough for the expression of it.

Sarah climbed a small ridge that was the entry point to the valley of Megiddo, she remembered the aftermath of the battle that was not. Ringing in her ears was the awful sound of thousands of birds ripping the flesh of those who had longed to attack God. That day, she had wanted to get away from there as quickly as she could. As she rounded the top of the ridge and the valley slumbered before her, Sarah was awestruck. There before her, over a bed of pallid, crushed bones, rose the most beautiful array of flowers than she had ever seen on Earth. They were tall, reaching forth with a myriad of colors. It was like a glorious bouquet, five or 6 miles long and at least 3 miles wide. The aroma of so many varieties of flowers, she wondered if she could even enumerate them, burst forth with loveliness. It was incredible!

Sarah sat down, stretching her feet out in front of her, and rested contemplatively. She released the memory of her first visit to the valley and eased into the beauty of life arrayed before her and ahead of her. Soaking in the beauty exhibited before her, she pondered that her portion of the ministry, which she was about to embark upon to the young believers, would be one of encouraging and affirming in a concrete way, the eternal truths that Jesus would be sharing. She attentively inquired of the Spirit, the specifics for the first meeting, so that she would be able to effectively prepare for her role. After asking, Sarah simply waited, with her eyes still closed, but her senses open to everything around her. She breathed in of the fragrance wafting throughout the valley. She heard the swishing sounds of a myriad of tiny birds and butterflies that flitted about as they stuffed themselves on the sweet nectar of abundance.

The Spirit of the Lord whispered to Sarah, first of His love for her, then the details of the upcoming meeting. "I will be sharing two main points, first, that in Me, what has been horrible in life, will be transformed to be beautiful blessings."

Sarah needed a moment, for her mind to comprehend The Spirit speaking to her in the first person, I, when He spoke of what Jesus would share with the group. It seemed to Sarah that intellectually, she comprehended the fact that The Father, The Son, and The Spirit *really are one*, but now she was experiencing the reality of it in everyday life. It caught her off-guard for a moment, making her head spin. As soon as it came upon her, she felt the Lord's love stabilizing her head and stopping the spinning feeling. With a renewed sense of the physical Presence of God with her, Sarah realized that the place to which she was drawn was an exact representation of what Jesus would be sharing. The horrible memory of seeing all the carcasses of unbelievers and their horses upgraded to joy, as she feasted her eyes on the floral panorama before her.

The Spirit affirmed her insight and even went a step further, "Indeed, it was the minerals of their bones that fed the flowers and caused such tremendous growth. This leads me to the second point I will be sharing, that I utilize the most difficult things to cause profound growth. In the case of this valley, the innermost parts of the unbelievers' bodies fed the plants with their minerals."

It seemed a bit gross to Sarah, thinking about the innards of thousands of people causing the lush floral abundance that lay before her. But then, she remembered how, when she was living on Earth the first time, it was in the brokenness in her innermost being that God poured His grace into and blessed her. It became the source of personal growth, which God used to help others who were hurting to heal. These two truths and how they combined to lay a foundation for a life of faith captivated Sarah. She asked the Lord, "How can I assist You in this initial gathering?"

"With tender encouragement," the Spirit whispered in her ear (His words even reverberated to the inner core of her body). "Remember the ice-breaker and how so many people were blessed in the simple act of sharing?" Sarah did remember, with great joy. "I would like you to lead this group in sharing with each other through this exercise. It will be a way for a sense of community to develop within the group. Then, as we walk to this valley, I will share my teaching and the power of it will be before their eyes, when they survey this bounty, as it has been for you this morning."

"Oh yes, Lord, I would love to do the ice-breaker! In every group I've led, this activity has opened hearts and minds to the profound beauty of Your Presence in our lives. Thank you for the honor of serving you and yours in this way. I'll head home now and prepare!" With that, Sarah took a huge breath, sucking into her lungs all the luscious fragrance she could muster and turned away to head home. She loved this new opportunity to give of herself to meet the needs of others! She was so enthusiastic; she picked up the pace and broke into an all-out sprint!

Chapter 3
Ruminating and Preparing

Sarah loved the run home; she felt so exhilarated by the warm air flying through her loosely-braided hair and was hardly even breathless when she arrived back at her abode. Stepping into the comfortable living room, she breathed deep of the fragrance of her ribbon rose bouquet. For a moment, she queried in her mind, "How can ribbon roses be so delightfully fragrant?"

A mere moment later, she received from The Gentle Spirit, the answer and giggled at its simple truth, "With God, all things are possible! This fragrant bouquet will never lose its scent, nor fade in beauty."

Sarah replied with a joyful pirouette, "Of course, my Lord will continue to bless me. Your blessings are eternal. Thank you, praise always be to your name!" With a smile that hinted of her delight, she began to focus on the ice breaker activity for the morning assemblage. Since she had shared this particular activity so many times, she barely had to think about the preparation. She pulled an enormous picnic tray out from a kitchen cupboard, set it on the dining table and proceeded to gather seemingly insignificant knick-knacks from around the house. Candles, puzzle pieces, kitchen gadgets, small household tools, little artistic decorative pieces, sewing aids, and even pretty rocks and ocean shells all found space on the tray.

When at length Sarah was satisfied that she had enough variety, she took time to rest and have a bite to eat. Munching on a toasted bagel with cream cheese, she thought, "*I sure enjoy eating, but I love that my body doesn't need food, or sleep, with the intensity that it had before Resurrection Morning. That great boost of energy I feel after eating just a bit, or resting even the tiniest of moments, is so uplifting! I don't even think of time the same way, because day or night, all day every day and all night every night, I live in the Presence of the Living God. Time no longer matters to me; however, it sure is very much a part of the lives of the people who lived through the Tribulation time on Earth.*" She reflected, "*Therefore, I will consider it important to me, to more graciously interact with everyone.*"

After eating, Sarah went outdoors, glided onto a well-worn, yet beautiful porch lounger and relaxed in the warmth of the afternoon. Her thoughts drifted backward in time, over the days since coming back to Earth. As she rambled through memories, she asked the Lord God to reveal the spiritual truths that she may have missed, in the manner that she had learned from Keturael, She reposed her senses, closing her eyes, allowing even the warmth of the day to recede from her awareness, and finally, calming her inquisitive, organizational mind. She breathed in deeply, "Abba," then held her breath for a moment and breathed out, "Father." Then, focusing her mind on the spiritual, she opened herself totally to the Spirit. With her eyes closed and her heart and mind open, the Lord revealed much more than what she remembered of those first days on Earth.

Sarah remembered feeling like she was in a blur of activity, first that spiritually intense battle in the valley of Megiddo, then walking to the uninhabited city of Jerusalem. As the first homes and businesses came into view, Jesus had paused, turned to His beloved and said, "It seems that those who occupied these dwellings and commerce are no more. As my Spirit leads each of you, be blessed to dwell and activate commerce with peace and joy."

Sarah recalled how the throng walked together and as they went, they heard the voice of the Spirit, announcing each dwelling and the one to be blessed in it. The businesses were also given, as each were in total alignment with individual skills and interests. There were no unpleasant interactions, only the blessings of the Lord for His people. Even after Sarah had received her Earth

Dwelling, and explored its beauty, she heard the Spirit dispersing individuals throughout the city. She also heard the praises going up to the Father, to Jesus, and to the Spirit from grateful hearts.

Sarah remembered feeling a bit strange making herself at home in someone else's home. She smiled as she recalled how precious the Spirit's words were, "I too am grieved for those who inhabited this city. Each person is so dear to my heart. My virtue respects fully their choices; therefore, if the one who lived in this abode chose to receive Jesus' gift of salvation, this abode would still be his. I bless this home to you; release any feeling of uneasiness." Sarah was indeed blessed living there. The rugged beauty of the Mideast dwellings wrought a sense of lifelong worship; Sarah had immersed herself in its allure.

A little bug made his way up Sarah's leg. Rather than flicking it aside, she looked at it with renewed wonder, for God created even the bugs to be blessed. She lifted the tiny creature up on her finger and looked at it, crawling this way and that on the tip of her finger. She smiled and it jumped up and down, then unfolded hidden wings and flew off – surprising Sarah so much she jumped! She reflected upon the physical changes that Jesus had made in the environment; they were so complete that it truly astounded Sarah. There had never in all of history, been a cleansing of the air, Earth, and water so profound, as when Jesus personally cleansed the Earth He created. It felt so clean to breathe in unpolluted air, and eat chemical-free fruit. Sarah recalled how the plants, water, and air had first responded to the very Presence of Jesus, the Creator, becoming healthy, clean, robust and more beautiful. In the early weeks, Jesus encircled the Earth, removing the unhealthy chemicals, garbage, and waste, sending them all to oblivion. He alone is Creator; He alone is able to extinguish. After that first season of adjustment, Sarah had explored and engorged her senses on the beauty of the Earth, which through Christ was restored to the fullness it was created to be. Earth itself had groaned under the weight of humanity's polluting ways, waiting for the day of its redemption; now it rejoiced! Sarah was breathless with the powerful beauty of this land of plenty.

She lifted up her arms and hands, praising God for His perfect care of her and of all her brothers and sisters in Christ. She twirled among the flowers that grew unassisted and flourishing all around her abode and among nearby homes and businesses. Sarah glanced a bit to the right, and coming over the miniscule incline were familiar red curls bouncing in the wind; it was her mentor in faith and dear friend, Sally. Sarah erupted in a holler and ran to hug her dear friend. As they embraced, they both felt the warmth of God's blessing making their entire bodies tingle.

Amidst that grace-laden tingle, they felt and heard the Lord's affirmation, "I have chosen Sally to work with you, Sarah; you both have abundant abilities and copious compassion."

Sally confirmed, "I am so glad we have been chosen and blessed by God. Let's begin with prayer, to consecrate our time and energy for His glory and honor."

Sarah nodded and they sat upon the comfortable lounge chairs in the front yard, held hands and prayed, silently at first; then Sarah finished up, "Father God, our Savior Jesus, and our wonderful Counselor, unite us in your love and purpose. Help us to be more together than either of us would be on our own; for You are with us always. Bring out the gifting that you placed in each of us in such a unique way that people will be blessed. Help us to be mentors of faith, as Sally so faithfully has been for me, and bond us as a tightly woven tapestry with those whom you lift up in your grace. We thank you Father God, for the gracious opportunity to encourage the people you love. We give you all the glory, in the matchless Name of Jesus, Amen."

Sally echoed enthusiastically, "Amen!" then asked Sarah about her morning. "I have had such a fascinating morning! I was wondering how your morning was? I just know it was way beyond the ordinary, Please tell me all the details and then I'll tell you what happened to me!"

Sarah told her about the dream of the ribbon morphing into flowers, but realized it was more than a dream and renamed it for what it truly was, a vision. She then told her of the stunning fulfillment of it, just as the vision faded, with Jesus' visit and His gift of the exquisite ribbon rose bouquet. She exclaimed, "I never knew ribbon could be so delicate and beautiful! And the really funny part was the aroma, a profound, heady fragrance that was like thousands of roses, all packed tightly into this bouquet of ribbon roses."

Sally leaned toward Sarah and spilled out the blessings that flowed, "Just now, as I was listening, the Holy Spirit showed me that it is the actual fragrance that The Father receives from your worship and prayer."

The Spirit gently whispered "The ribbon bouquet is for you to have throughout eternity, to rejoice in us as we rejoice in you. The fragrance will increasingly bless you, as your worship and prayer continually blesses us."

"Wow! This is so wonderful," Sarah sighed, as the familiar tingling of the Presence of the Holy Spirit washed over her body. Sally nodded in agreement, also feeling His Presence and held her friend's hands in fellowship.

"My experience this morning was also very powerful and profound," Sally said with a look of awe radiating all over her face. "I love to take early morning walks around the beautiful countryside surrounding Jerusalem. The olive groves are so fragrant and the hills are covered with fields of grain and fruit groves intermixed with delicate flowers bordering each farm. I often walk for a couple of hours just filling my senses with the goodness of God's creation. I let go of myself in worship, and feel that absolute blessing of the Spirit wash over my body.

"This morning, I began my walk earlier than usual, just as the sun was rising over the hills surrounding Jerusalem. It was so beautiful. I just stopped and held that moment close, fixing my mind to be like a camera, stopping everything around me to embrace the newness of the morning, the warmth of a new day and the life-giving hope that we have in Christ Jesus.

"I heard the audible voice of the Father calling me to newness of life, to a new purpose that will give Him glory. He said to me in His deep resonating base voice, 'My dear Sally, you are my beloved; you have honored me with faithfulness in teaching the children about faith and life in Jesus. I have prepared a new ministry of love and encouragement and have given you the abilities and sensitivity to accomplish this well. Jesus will be teaching those who are babes in the faith, who received my Son in the years of tribulation and survived the days of evil-run-amuck. You have been an encourager, a mentor, and have brought your atypical sense of humor into all of life, the physical, emotional, and spiritual. Will you accompany Sarah, in leading activities, which will galvanize the truths that Jesus will share in my dear ones' lives? I will be with you, guiding you along the way, and will bless your efforts.'

"I quickly responded, 'Oh my, yes! I would love to, Father, It is an honor that you would have me share in this endeavor. Thank you. I love you so; I love being with you and living in your Presence. I want to thank you for this odd sense of humor you've given me. I love having fun in all of life!'

"Father God replied, with deep love in His voice, 'I want to bless you in such a way that you will never have any question about your call. My love will pour over you, NOW.' "

Sally could hardly say the words; the memory of what happened enveloped her so much. She breathed out the words, "I felt His love wash over me like a river and was carried away in its flow of love. I was covered, cleansed, and consecrated. I lost myself in the majestic Presence of God. I lost all track of time, place, and even my body in the absolute love that swathed me. The river of love slowly receded and soaked into the soil, whereupon a sweet bed of wildflowers sprang to life all around me. I just laid back upon their soft blossoms and breathed deeply of their diverse fragrances, which together filled my nostrils with aromatic joy. I lay there on the bed of wildflowers for quite a while, pondering and still receiving the profound love of God. When I arose, I felt the Spirit silently guiding me to come to your abode and; He will guide both of us into His perfect will." As she finished her soliloquy, Sally breathed in deep and exhaled with a "Wow!"

Sarah reached for Sally and hugged her fiercely. Unhurriedly releasing her friend, Sarah exhaled deeply and said, "Oh my, how wonderful! I too was surrounded with flowers that thrived, on my hike to the Valley of Megiddo this afternoon. It is almost as if the Lord is showing us the beauty of His creation that will flourish through our efforts. This is a significant task which we have been given. The first activity that the Lord inspired me to prepare for is a fun ice breaker, which will help those in the group to know each other more. Each time I have utilized it, the Holy Spirit has blessed everyone in the group immensely. It is a very simple task of relating where you are as an individual, physically, spiritually, or even emotionally, with an object that you choose from many objects. For example, I might say that, 'In my life right now, I am like this reclining chair. I'm ready to be used and am content to wait until God brings the right person, who may need rest and recuperation.' This activity provides an open door for each individual to express their hope, confusion, inadequacy, whatever it is that they are experiencing. The rest of the group merely listens and accepts their declarations. So, this afternoon, I have gathered a bunch of the items I think we will need. Let's go in and take a look to evaluate if we have enough."

With their arms draped over each other's shoulders, Sarah and Sally went into the small dwelling. Upon entering the living room, Sally said, "Ah, this is indeed a beautiful bouquet; it smells delightful!"

Sarah responded, "It sure does! The fragrance fills the entire house, but it is the loveliest in here." Shifting her attention to the upcoming activity and guiding Sally to the dining room, she continued, "I have all the things I could think of for the ice breaker on this platter. Do you think we will need any more?"

Sally did a quick calculation just by glancing over the items. "I see about 50 or 60 items here," she said, "but I think it might be good to have a gardening tool and perhaps a small mirror. Oh, and what do you think about a toy, like a stuffed animal? The items could be used by more than one individual, if needed."

"That sounds great," Sarah replied, giggling at the idea of a stuffed animal. "I think I have a small mirror in the bathroom. I don't use that room much, anymore. It's so nice that our bodies don't have to eliminate anything anymore!" She went to look and brought back an diminutive oval mirror, adding it to the tray and making sure it didn't break as she set it down. She motioned to another room, revealing to her friend, "I have a stuffed bear that I enjoy cuddling with. Would you like to head in there and get him, while I go outside and look in my gardening bin for a hand trowel?"

"Sure, I can do that!" Sally quipped, as she headed to the side room. The cute little bear lay on the lounger, and Sally thought, "It's sitting there, as if reposing was its favorite activity!" She scooped it up, cuddling it close and smiling broadly. Just as she set the bear onto the tray, Sarah popped in the door, carrying two hand tools for gardening, a trowel, which looked a bit like a scoop, and a tiller that had three claw-like protrusions to loosen the soil.

Sarah exclaimed, "It looks good! I think we have just the right amount. What do you think, Sally?"

"I agree," Sally responded. "I know the blessings will pour down, as droplets of sweet joy, when we do this activity! I'm looking forward to it!"

Sarah declared, "Me too!" They decided to relax over large cups of steaming tea and once again committing the ice breaker to the Lord. They were both so full of the Lord's love that it was a challenge for both of them to be patient and wait until the morning hours. They visited, thankful that their bodies no longer needed 6 to 8 hours of sleep every night. They reminisced about their families, how each one made the transition to Earth living again.

Sally shared, "My brood is all spread out, but they are all so delighted to be living here with the Lord Jesus. We always longed to visit the Holy Land, as we used to call it." (They both giggled) "Now, the entire Earth is the Holy Land! Life is so very blessed now, especially when we think about how life used to be, with the news filled daily with multiple murders, attacks, and sexual deviancy." Shifting a bit in her dialog, Sally continued, "Recently, I've spent a lot of time with Rob; it is fascinating to me how our marriage transformed into this deeper, more profound relationship. We are closer now; he is able to sense my emotions and respond to my need even before I know myself what my need is! Even though were are not physically intimate, our relationship is so passionate, I can hardly describe it. It is truly an expression of the intimacy between us and our triune God."

"I agree entirely," Sarah avowed. "Paul and I have had the most delightful times together. We enjoy each other at a deeper level; I don't even know how we got there! I truly think God scooped out all the heartaches that we caused each other and sent them packing. In their place, the Lord has filled in with such a profound passion that whenever we're together, a warmth of love flows over and through us."

"Exactly," Sally responded. "Recently, I had the opportunity to visit with Eve, the first of womanhood. She shared with me, when I talked with her about this passion, that this is how she felt on Earth, with Adam in the Garden of Eden and with God in their lives every day. She said when they sinned, the physical intimacy no longer was a part of the real passion; it became only a hint of what they both had with God. She said it was most intriguing that now, with God's everlasting presence with us, the passion exists without the need, or desire for that matter, for physical intimacy. In fact, she and Adam experience the same passion as you and Paul, and me and Rob. The sweetness of God's intimacy is with us, without the need or encumbrances of marriage, as it was on Earth."

"How wonderful that you visited with Eve!" exclaimed Sarah. "I love visiting with people of faith from all epochs on Earth. The other day, I visited with Hannah, Samuel's mother. My, is she a woman of faith! It was exhilarating to see her hopes and dreams fulfilled by our God. She is no longer the barren woman that her culture held as such a blight to her human existence, before her deep prayer and God's gracious answer. Indeed, she is a woman of extra-ordinary grace; it oozes out her entire countenance!" Sarah snickered a bit at her own words, but it was true! "I feel like living in the presence of the Lord is such a blessed place to be. Moreover, living in the midst of His faithful followers from all eons is absolute utopia."

"It sure is!" confirmed Sally. "Rob has also been meeting with men and women from every epoch. He is working on a magnificent testimony of the faithful, a written volume that will highlight miracles throughout humanity, that all may know of the enormity of God's love and grace to us. I am so thankful for him in my life. My kids," she interrupted herself with "Don't we always think of them as our kids? They are having a great time too, visiting with those of every century; they are maturing even more in the faith because of it! Ted is fitting right in with his construction skills. Here on Earth, there's always the need for skilled tradesmen for renovations and new structures. Ron is ever the naturalist, leading explorations near and far. My crazy one, Bill is taking on the sweetest ministry, helping those who are challenged by the change back to living on Earth once again. There is an adjustment needed, even though our bodies have changed so drastically from what they were. And there are questions a-flying, like how is it that our bodies have changed, but those who received the Lord during the Tribulation, here on Earth, haven't changed. I think he has his hands full! I'm thankful the Lord is with him, pouring His grace over all His people. My sweet Anna is partnering with many women of faith to make sure the physical needs of the people, such as food, water, and a place to live, are satisfied. With more and more new believers coming in from around the entire Earth, there is such a huge hustle and bustle around here!"

"Absolutely, Sarah responded. "I've been giving myself a bit of time to get used to all the changes myself! I think that's why I haven't jumped into ministry myself. But you know? Jesus knew that I needed that time and He prepared me, and you too, Sally, for this very special ministry to new believers."

At that, Sarah observed that their tea was gone and went about mixing up fruit smoothies. Bringing them to the table, she set them down, set herself down and briefly caressed her sister's hand. It was such a small movement, yet blessed both of them more than either expected. It felt as if there was more of a connection than she had ever had with any other friend, a very special bond that God forged between them.

Sally felt the strength of that bond too, and remarked, "Oh, God is doing something profound here; I am not sure, but it feels like we've just been bound together for the grace of God to move powerfully through us."

Sarah agreed, "It sure does! It felt like we were magnetized and when we are near each other, the pull will be strong, for His glory. Wow! That's huge!"

Sarah nodded with deep emotion and, after taking a deep breath, commented about her family, "My kids too, have jumped in energetically – they have so much vim and vigor! Mark is such a gifted artist; he is teaching youngsters in the artistic expression of worship, both in paint and dance. John is seeking the Lord every day, to follow Him and serve his Lord. I am especially honored in his humble devotion. He is in a theatric group which explores in Poetic Theater especially the love of God, but other subjects as well.

"My precious Linda is playing with the little ones, the very young children – reading to them and singing fun gospel and folk songs. She loves plays with them and caring for them, all with giggles and fun spread all over her face. She is even applying her gymnastics as a fun way to teach children to care for and enjoy these wonderful bodies that God gave us. She loves her new life in the Lord. He gave her a powerful ability and love for helping children."

"And now to my dear brother, who was my husband not so long ago." Momentarily taking a side tangent, Sarah exclaimed, "It seems now like a lifetime ago!" Then, back on track with her original theme, "When Paul is not exploring the beauty of music playing in the orchestra, he is leading a group of men, in which the older brothers of faith mentor the younger ones."

"My, oh my!" Sally observed. "The Lord is blessing so much! Everything changed on that wonderful Resurrection Morning. It was just as is described in the Word of God, "in the twinkling of an eye!" And now, to be back on Earth, with Jesus and all His power and love surrounding every aspect of our lives, is so much more than I ever could have imagined."

The two ladies, who had years ago been merely trailer park neighbors, visited long into the night – giggling at the many years of memories they had together. They were no longer old women, but vibrant, energetic, and so full of joy they could hardly contain it all.

Sally began to notice the sky lighting up, first with pale light and then bright pink and red as the sun popped up over the horizon. She smiled and exclaimed "We have talked the night away! We should pray and eat a bit and gather these things and head to the meeting!"

Sarah agreed and they grasped each other's hands and with Sarah leading, prayed, "Our Father, we thank you for this beautiful night of sharing and rejoicing together about all the blessings you have showered over us. Be with us today, as we partner with you to encourage and build up your precious family. Lord, we ask you to bless this ice breaker activity to everyone's heart; may it be a beautiful launching point for the group. We thank you Father, for our lives, which have been transformed by your grace, to bring you glory. In the mighty name of our Lord Jesus, Amen."

The two ladies slurped quickly their fruit smoothies, munched on quiche and sweet rolls, and gathered up the tray, each of them grasping a handle. It wasn't a heavy tray, but was a bit bulky and would have been a challenge for only one person to carry. Maneuvering through the diminutive cottage and out the front door, they embarked upon the short walk to the community center, as the Spirit had whispered to them both, of the place and time. They had barely set out the items for the activity, spreading them all over a large, 6 ft. x 2.5 ft. table, when the room swelled with men and women, boys and girls. Jesus came in, meandering peacefully, hugging and blessing every person, even Sarah and Sally. Anticipation filled the room; the cognizance of imminent blessing, renewal, growth, and ministry hung heavy in the air.

Chapter 4
Breaking the Ice - Blessings Flow

Jesus stepped to the front of the room and commenced, "It is my joy to welcome you this morning, to our first 'Rising in Faith' meeting. At each of our meetings, we will have two parts, the first - 'Focus on Faith' in which I will teach principles of living and growing in my grace. The second will be an activity, which will reinforce in practical ways the principle I present. Some of the activities will be outside this room, but each will be a blessings to you. I am always available to you for questions and my Spirit will also be with us, guiding each of you personally and intimately into fullness of blessings through the grace of Our Father God, myself and our Spirit.

Continuing, Jesus introduced his assistants, "I have asked Sarah and Sally, (who both stood up) to help me with activities that will compliment every teaching. Father God, Myself, and Our Spirit has given each individual unique gifts, which in the fullness of Our grace and love, are utilized and blessed for the uplifting of the whole family of God.

"This morning," Jesus mentioned, "We are going to have the activity first, then we will go on a walk together." Lifting his arms Heavenward, Jesus blessed the morning's event, "Father, You have given me these dear ones. The flow of blessings is ever outward from us, we bless these people for your glory, Amen." When Jesus spoke "Amen," sweet dew droplets flowed down upon everyone in the room, including Jesus. He huskily shared, "This is the blessing of the Father, through the power of the Spirit. Even I am blessed, as you, in His love." The 500 or so, who had gathered for the meeting, were all flushed and emotionally satiated and the morning had hardly begun!

Sarah rose and began to share about the introductory activity, "We are sharing with you these fun, thought-provoking activities that will bless all of us. This first one will give you the opportunity to share about your life. We will begin to know each other in a way that is unique. On this table are a variety of items. I would like a few of you at a time, to come and look at these and each of you choose one which will represent something about your life, where you are now. It is OK to share the positives and also the negatives of your life. I will go first, to give you an idea of how to do this. Remember, this is about you, so there is no way that you will say or do anything wrong. This takes a bit of courage, to stand before others and share parts of your life, but the blessings that come from this are well worth the challenge."

Sarah went to the table, and picked up a cobalt blue, glass napkin holder. She held it up so everyone could see and began to share, "I'm Sarah; my life right now is like this napkin holder. I know I'm beautiful because God has made me so." Sarah paused for the humor to soak in. When she heard a few snickers, she continued, "I am open to God using me; I'm ready for His purposes to be fulfilled in my life. He is placing within this open space," she indicated with her hand, the space for the napkins, "challenges for me to fulfill. One of those is being here, doing this!" and she spread her arms and placed the napkin holder back on the table, as she finished her example, "Now it is your turn. Please, about 3 at a time, come up to the table and choose something here that you can use to describe your life right now. Tell us your name, and using one of the items on the table, about your life right now. There is no wrong thing to say, so wonderful things and difficult, even awful things are allowed. We are in the very presence of Grace, our Lord Jesus." And she waived her arm broadly toward Jesus and he bowed slightly in acknowledgement; Sarah sat down, and

Sally stood and indicated for the first three to come up and peruse the table.

A tall, slim fella, with thick, bushy hair chose a large puzzle piece from a child's puzzle and shared, "My name is George. My life has been so fractured, it felt like a puzzle with a thousand pieces, pieces that I couldn't fit together. I felt broken and sad. Ever since I received Jesus as my Savior, the pieces have been coming together, each fitting into the right spot and helping me to feel a wonderful peace. Coming here and living with you, Jesus, is like the last piece of the puzzle has fit into its proper place; I am completely fulfilled." George went to his seat amid lively applause.

The second to share was a short lady with a tiny face that sported a huge smile. In fact, it seemed as though her whole face was smiling! Her eyes effervesced with joy. In a quiet voice that spoke of her natural shyness, she spoke, "My name is Muriel." She held up a rolling pin (used to flatten dough for cookies and pies) and quipped, "I used to feel like people were rolling all over me, flattening me until I thought I was almost nothing. I know now that Jesus had something else in mind; He transformed the awful deeds of those who hurt me into a humility and compassion for other people who have suffered. Now, I am able to see a rolling pin and be thankful for that process of teaching me to listen to Him, to seek His face. Now, I am fully able to see you, Jesus. My honor is given to you," she ended, with the rolling pin pointing to Jesus, as she bowed her head in adoration. She then returned to her seat, amidst boisterous applause.

As Sally motioned for the next three more individuals to rise and scan the table, a redheaded fellow, complete with freckles splattering his face and arms, held up an iron. "My name is Sandy. My mom used to use one of these every week to press our clothes for church. I was so confused because it seemed like no matter how clean and pressed I looked on the outside, I knew I was dirty and ugly on the inside. Seeing this iron brought me back to the person I was, putting on a front for people to see. Then, one day, I learned about having a relationship with this Jesus we had only talked about. I received Him into my heart and have been growing ever since. And now, Jesus, my wonderful Savior and buddy! I'm yours!" In his exuberance, Sandy ran over to Jesus and jumped into His embrace. The room erupted in applause.

When everything died down again, a stunningly beautiful middle-aged lady began to share, "My name is Bridgett. "I've chosen a whisk, because most of my life there has been such turmoil. I grew up a city, Berlin, which was divided both physically and emotionally. When I was a teenager, the wall that had separated family and friends for years came down. There was a lot of pain involved in that wall; it took time for the wounds to even begin to heal. I felt like my life was mixed up to the point that I didn't even know who I was. When the Lord came into my life, I was restored to wholeness. Everything came to a great peace, deep in my soul. Now, I feel like I'm being whisked a bit, moving, coming to a new place and a new life. But it is a good feeling, because I am filled with this powerful love and nothing can hurt me again. I am loved and am so very thankful, Lord Jesus," and she bowed low to give Him the glory for all He had done for her. When she arose and made her way back to her seat, there were calls of "Amen" and "Praise God" that followed her.

Waves of transformed individuals surged throughout the day, each sharing about their lives, using the tangible focus of everyday items as a springboard. They took a short hiatus for lunch, then jumped right back into the stories. Some were comical, like the fellow who used a simple ice cream scoop to show very graphically how the Lord scooped him apart from the life of sin that he had been involved in. Even as he introduced himself, Kevin's hands and arms were flying all over. He lifted high the scoop and in a sweeping motion, almost like a tractor scoop, he described himself being absolutely removed from the barb of sin. Pulling the lever that releases the ice cream from the scoop, Kevin turned the scoop upside-down and he said, "Plop! I am in the place of God's Grace, because I have believed in His son, Jesus Christ! I have a new life of righteousness, trusting in you, Jesus, for everything!" Peals of laughter broke out and applause followed Kevin, as he raised his hand toward Jesus and honored Him who makes all things new.

There were some poignant moments, such as when a jet-black haired lady, Maria, shared how her life was as a beautiful paperweight. She told of the heaviness of her soul, physical pain that she had endured from severe multiple sclerosis, but also shared the beauty it forged in her soul. She expressed how the love of the Lord Jesus comforted her and helped her to endure the daily discomforts of MS. She then shared, "When I first received Jesus into my heart and soul, He healed the emotional part of me that was broken. He reversed the effect of my own sin, which had come in the form of bitterness and anger. I felt so clean that I was emotionally stronger and able to endure the fact that my body still hurt. I had no idea, Jesus, how much You would bless me. I arrived here just a few weeks ago and You came to me and healed every cell of my body. I no longer have MS!" (Great applause surged!) "So now, this beautiful paperweight is like me it its beauty. But I am more; I am not limited to staying in one place. The Lord will move me around His body for His purpose and glory. I am very thankful, Jesus, for your continuing love!" Applause reverberated, as Jesus bowed following to her tribute.

At length, when everyone had shared and friendships were emerging, Jesus stood once again and thanked Sarah and Sally for assisting. He was mindful that the folks still needed rest and sleep. He dismissed the group with this blessing and teaser for the morrow, "My love flows to you now and ever more. Prepare your hearts for new expressions of my love and provision. Amen." Rippling "Amens" floated around the room. Individuals began to rise and hug each other in newfound affinity. Sarah and Sally began to gather up the items, putting them on Sarah's platter once again. They were both surprised that so many people came up to them and thanked them for the day, chock-full of blessings because of the intriguing activity. Jesus too, was surrounded; He blessed His beloved over and over, with precious hugs and miraculous words over them.

Presently, the room emptied and only Jesus, Sarah, and Sally remained. Jesus hugged them both tenderly, whispering in their ears of His love and blessing upon them both. He released them with, "Until tomorrow then, my love go with you both." Sarah and Sally both flushed with the joy of His love. Each of them took ahold of a handle on the tray and began the short trek back to Sarah's abode.

Along the way, they discussed how beautifully the activity progressed throughout the day. Sally could hardly hold in her amazement, "I've been in many groups in which this ice-breaker activity was used, but today, it was as if the very fulfillment of God's ultimate purpose was accomplished. I was in awe that in every case, Jesus was the focus of honor and glory, for He alone has been the worker of all the miracles in every one of their lives. It was so very profound!"

Sarah nodded and replied, "I too was in awe of the transformation of all of their lives. It is so precious to now be living in the very presence of Jesus. I remember longing for this to happen, way back before Resurrection Morning. I think being a part of this group, sharing the activities the Spirit places in our hearts, will be such a powerful work of grace and love. I am absolutely stoked!"

At that, Sally guffawed, throwing her head back with all her carefree, red curls rebounding in a lively whirl. She affirmed, "I am too! What a beautiful day it has been, to honor Jesus and see how much it blesses Him!"

As they arrived to Sarah's Earth abode, Sarah asked, "Would you like a bite to eat? I have some luscious fruit." She placed the large platter, filled with fresh fruit on the table and Sally simply nodded and sank into a chair.

She acknowledged, "I think I need to gather myself a bit. When these blessings come, they are so huge my head feels like its spinning and I have to rest, just to calm down and ease into the flow of God's blessings."

Sarah let out a huge "ahhh" as she gathered the fruit and cut it into manageable chunks. She continued, "I understand completely and agree entirely. A day full of the blessings of God can be exceptionally intense. I think some food will help, just to do something mundane for a while. How about a short hike after we eat, just for some fun?" Sarah finished as she handed Sally a plate and fork and took one of each for herself.

"That sounds dandy!" Sally responded as they both munched pineapple, apple and banana chunks. "Ron took me on a fabulous hike in the wilderness beyond the environs of Jerusalem. He showed me a short hike, but indicated that there are many levels of hiking, from the slightest of effort to the most strenuous of hikes into steep terrain. I think it will be just the thing to shift from the deeply emotional time we had today, to a hike into the grandeur of God's creation.

"Oh, I'm excited to explore," Sarah said. "It's wonderful that Ron is a tour guide. He is so gracious with people." With her last bite, she sighed and leaned back in her lounger and quipped, "I sure love eating for pleasure. I'm so blessed by our forever bodies, that we can no longer abuse them, nor do we want to! So, are you about ready to have some fun? I sure am!"

"You bet!" replied Sally, after swallowing her last bite of pineapple. With that, they both hopped out of their seats and bounded toward the door, playfully engaging in a race. "I win, I win!" hollered Sally. "I'm faster than you!"

"I think you had a head start!" exclaimed Sarah. But I have to concede; you are very fast!" The two ladies, who had first met in their mid-20's, matured in faith together as their children grew up, and experienced the aches and pains of growing old (before Resurrection Day) now bounded off together as youthful and exuberant as teenagers.

Chapter 5
Hiking Grandeur

Sally led the way; she knew that Sarah would love the rugged beauty of the wilderness. They followed a dirt path that sported multitudinous travelers walking upon it. As they ambled along, they observed the foliage that lined the path with beauty abundant. The gals chatted, about the profusion of floral colors, shapes, and scents. Sally proclaimed, "I want to just bury my face in all the blossoms and breathe in deep of their luxurious aromas."

Sarah added her two-cents in, "God's beauty constantly surrounds us now. Jesus not only healed the Earth of all the horrible pollution, but has released all the trees, shrubs, and flowers to a vitality that I've never seen! Now that I think about it, He even has blessed the Earth itself with vigor, removing the vestiges of sin from its grip upon every aspect of life on Earth. The rocks and hills, dirt and water, all sing glory to God, within the framework of their own capacity to do so. You know," she continued, "I think that if we are open to interact with what we thought were inanimate objects, we may even be able to join with them in exuberant worship!"

"Oh my!" responded Sally. "I have never even thought about that. As we walk, let's ask the Spirit to show us how to connect with things in nature, to worship God together."

"Yes," Sarah affirmed. She grasped her dear friend's hand and lifted it, and her own, heavenward and launched, "Father, we are still learning of your grace in creation. We are both in awe of the beauty that surrounds us; and yet there is more than just beauty. We have begun to more fully grasp that even the rocks sing out your praises! All of nature expresses your glory in a myriad of ways. Help us, Daddy, to see, hear, feel, and even participate in, this integrated worship of your splendor. Thank you for the ever-expanding knowledge, personal growth, and grace that you provide for us. What joy we experience! In the mighty name of Jesus, Amen."

Sally responded with her own "Amen!" and bounded along the trail with even more gusto, almost dragging-in-tow her friend. She slowed down only to share the reason for such exuberance, "As you prayed, the Spirit prompted my heart to move quickly along the path, for He wanted our first experience to be the sunset and worship of the wilderness hills." With that, she let go of Sarah's hand and started once again in a full-out run, which served to entice Sarah into duplicating Sally's rapid gait. They both ran over the well-beaten path on into the rocky wilderness, where Jesus went before his first public ministry began. At first, there were just pebbles on the path, then a lessening of the abundant foliage amongst boulders on both sides of the trail, and finally, huge rocky crags that rose above the trail on both sides and ahead of the two gals. The crags became escarpments and Sally led the way up one of them, with Sarah following excitedly.

When Sally finally slowed down, Sarah stopped, stretched, and took a deep breath. When she released all the air she had drawn into her small frame, she looked at her friend and giggled. Sally was laying prostrate on the hard rock, with her cheek pressed against its warm, hard surface. Sarah queried, "Why are you laying down? I think I'm going to sit on this huge boulder," indicating a perfectly shaped bench-rock.

Sally explained, "When I arrived, the Spirit whispered to me that if I listen to the rock, very carefully, I would begin to feel the vibration of his praise. I do feel it; it's like a low rumble, a building up of unexpressed emotion. This is just the beginning! Wow! Now I'm OK to come and sit with you."

"Oh, I love taking in the absolute grandeur of this place," Sarah shared. "From this pinnacle, we can see all the other rocky crests that stretch out for miles. Look, there are groups of two and more people on so many of them! This is a place of profound beauty. And now, with the sun beginning its descent, the light is dancing on every hill and splashing the whole area with red, orange and yellow hues." Sarah broke out in spontaneous praise for God, singing luminously,

> "Fairest Lord Jesus, Ruler of all nature,
> O Thou of God and man the Son,
> Thee will I cherish, Thee will I honor,
> Thou, my soul's glory, joy and crown."

This first stanza Sarah sang alone, her strong alto voice echoing among the pinnacles. When she paused, Sally joined in, and then other voices began to rise – united in worship of The Lord Jesus from scraggly pinnacles near and far,

> "Fair are the meadows, fairer still the woodlands,
> robed in the blooming garb of spring;
> Jesus is fairer, Jesus is purer,
> who makes the woeful heart to sing.

> Fair is the sunshine,
> fairer still the moonlight,
> and all the twinkling starry host;
> Jesus shines brighter, Jesus shines purer
> than all the angels heaven can boast."

Then, as if a power seized the Earth itself, a deep vibration rose in earnest. The most profound facet was that the vibration became musical. The great beauty of the hymn, lifting praise to Jesus, was that it was expressed through the union of the voices of humanity and the musical vibrations of the Judean wilderness. Then a multitude of angels swept in, joining in with their voices, powerful and yet lofty, as if flowing in on the Mediterranean breeze.

> "All fairest beauty, heavenly and Earthly
> wondrously, Jesus, is found in Thee;
> none can be nearer, fairer or dearer,
> than Thou, my Savior, art to me.

New sounds added resounding and lively significance to the communal worship, animals braying, honking, twittering, and warbling. The animals did not detract the focus from worship, but unrestrainedly enhanced it.

> Beautiful Savior! Lord of all the nations!
> Son of God and Son of Man!
> Glory and honor, praise, adoration,
> now and forever more be Thine."

Sarah and Sally could hardly move, to take a breath, or even itch. Neither wanted the moment of penetrating unity of worship to be lessened. They both felt the Presence of the Spirit in their midst and were so blessed. The experience of worshipping God with believers atop other pinnacles - sprinkled all over the Judean wilderness as far as they could see, as well as the unity of worship with angelity and animality, was quite overwhelming. Amid the absolute beauty of the rugged Earth angles and their enraptured voices, they both felt and heard the praises of the Earth itself. All of life displayed their amassed awe of the Creator of all of life.

After holding the silence for long moments of personal worship, the ladies grew pensive of even what to say. Initially, Sally had thought the vibrating of the ground felt like a small Earthquake, but Sarah mentioned that it felt like the vibrator that her mother rubbed her sore legs with when she was a little girl and had roller-skated too long. Sally agreed and remarked that the low, rumbling sound of the Earth worshipping was like water whishing over rocks, gurgling in a low range, offering a foundational worship in which the human and angelic voices built upon. They shared back and forth about how profound of an experience it was.

Sarah seemed to hesitate for a moment in their conversation, trying to formulate her words, yet struggling a bit to express how she felt. Finally, she was able to articulate, "From when I was very young, I remember trying to explore worship. Once when I was laying down, in those moments before sleep, I prayed and asked my Lord to bless me. I didn't even know how He would, but I felt His joy at my request. Then, I began to feel a tingling, which started in my fingers, and then moved into my hands, then my arms and then all over my body. I felt His love wash over me like waves of a love so powerful that I could not experience it all. After languishing in the waves of love for a long while, I felt almost like I would burst if it continued. The Spirit knew my frailty and the waves of His powerful love began to subside. In the midst of this worship tonight, I felt that love wash over me again, wave after wave of His love, as we expressed our love and honor to Him."

The Spirit confirmed Sarah's memory in a warmly resonating tenor voice they both could hear. "Yes, my sweet Little One, it is within the expression of worship that the Father, Son and Myself are able to more fully share our love for humanity. It is not that we need to be worshipped, but rather it opens the human and angelic heart to receive our love into your spirit. The Earth, and all of the universe for that matter, has always been in tune with our love, for creation itself is an expression of our love. The Earth and sky and sea, as well as all the celestial bodies and individual atoms and molecules in the micro-universe, all worship continually and receive our love without ceasing. It is especially true, now that Jesus has removed from the Earth the effects of sin and its horrible consequences upon it. There is no longer decay upon the Earth, nor are there thorns, weeds, or noxious bugs nor toxic plants. Every living thing is as we have prepared it to be, for the glory of God and to bless all of humanity. Oh, how we love you!"

"Oh, thank you my Lord God," Sarah responded, then fell silent as she closed her eyes in silent prayer. Sally joined her friend in silent, inexpressible awe of the Triune God.

When they lifted their heads, with bright smiles lighting up their faces, Sally suggested they begin the trek back to the city. As they walked, she voiced more of her exhilaration of their worship. She began quietly, but gained confidence and intensity as her excitement ensued. "I first felt the worship when I followed The Spirit's prompting to lay down and listen. I had never even thought about the Earth worshipping God. I was confused about Jesus' declaration, way back when He was first mentoring His disciples; after the Pharisees demanded that Jesus rebuke His disciples' worship of Him, Jesus said, 'I tell you, if these become silent, the stones will cry out!' Until tonight, that verse befuddled me. I couldn't think beyond my box of secular education and life in a secular society. Even though I believed in Jesus Christ, I was unable to set aside the mundane of only seeing and enjoying plants and mountains and the stars; I could not imagine any one of them as perceiving and experiencing the Divine. Tonight, I had a huge lesson of exactly how profound is the expression of worship of all creation toward its Creator. It was life-changing! I feel united with all of humanity, angelity and nature. It is so much more than enjoying the flowers, trees and having fun with the animals; worship of our Lord God is powerful, delightful, and fills every pour of my body with awe. I feel like running again, how 'bout you?"

Sarah jumped into a run, as she responded in a boisterous holler, "You bet!" They sprinted all the way back to the city. As they plopped down on the lawn chairs at her abode, Sarah caught her breath and intoned, "I absolutely love having these bodies; they bear no pain, and we can run, jump, climb, swim, and wrestle with each other and with the animals, all without fear or concern of pain surging in!"

"Me too!" exclaimed Sally. She continued, "It's fun too, that we can accomplish so much more, since we no longer need to sleep a third of every day away! I was so blessed in our wilderness worship that I'm not even needing rest at all! Would you like to pray and ask the Lord about His upcoming lesson?"

Sarah replied, "I'm not tired either; the night of worship was invigorating! Now is a perfect time to prepare for the next step that we will be involved in." Grasping Sally's two hands in her own, Sarah led their prayer of inquiry and consecration of the upcoming day, "Thank you, Father God, for the glorious expression of our love and honor of you and how you blessed us both with your great love. Jesus, we are so thankful to be joining you in your blessing of new believers. How can we be of service to you today? Our hearts are open to whatever need there is. We'll just wait for a while, silent before your Presence, knowing you will reveal in your perfect timing how we can serve…."

As the two women bowed, the Spirit looked upon them and poured His love over them.

Chapter 6
The Kingdom of God

Sarah and Sally felt so refreshed after their prayer, but they had no idea of what the Lord had planned for the day.

The Spirit sang over them in a sweet tenor melody, "No eye has seen, no ear has heard, and no human mind has conceived the things God has prepared for those who love Him." Then he said, "Simply follow Jesus and soak in Truth; as the blessings unfold, I will show you how to serve the Savior and His people."

Sally and Sarah felt a palpable anticipation, as they picked peaches from a tree in Sarah's yard and slurped their way to the meeting hall. After a quick clean-up, they visited with the gathering group of people, which grew larger by the minute.

When Jesus entered, everyone quieted in eager expectation. He blessed them, reaching forth His hands as He spoke, "Today, you will begin to experience my Kingdom here on Earth. We will be taking a fun hike, to the valley of Megiddo, where you will see and feel the transformation of all that was negative into everything that is good and blessed." As He spoke, waves of love and blessing flowed from His hands and covering every person's head, like hot, clear wax poured over jam, sealing them – for they were His own. As the blessing settled upon everyone, audible "Ah's" echoed around the room.

With a discerning heart, Sarah knew that The Father, Jesus, and the Spirit were in unity of purpose and action. She treasured how the Triune God showed their love in so many ways. Jesus led the way out of the community center, with the group hanging around Him like an entourage, gathering participants as they rambled toward Megiddo.

There was no limitations on anything that Jesus was doing among the people. Anyone could join in, and many did, just because they knew when Jesus is nearby, blessings flow lavishly.

Jesus was in no hurry, for He was not bound by time. He welcomed each moment and utilized every minute in Divine purpose. His stride was relaxed and steady, yet He greeted those nearby by name and blessed each one. Sarah was not surprised then, that as they rounded the crest of the pass into the valley of Megiddo, there were thousands accompanying Jesus and those from the class. Jesus invited everyone to relax upon the flower-strewn valley. Children who had skipped along continued to play in the valley, rolling down the hillsides, which were carpeted with floral beauty.

Jesus began His object lesson, "Most of you remember the great battle that was in this beautiful valley, a mere 6 months ago. For the sake of those who were not here, I offer you this exercise. As a believer in God, you are able to learn this activity and experience any time in all of creation, not only as a flashback, so to speak, but when it actually happened. For some of you, this will be a new experience and therefore, a bit shocking. Behold…"

On a huge scale, almost as big as the valley itself, a replica of the valley appeared. Each person perceived it as if they were present at that time. The valley was filled with the hordes of unbelievers and Satan and the demons were shrinking back from Jesus. Jesus was at one end of the valley, with all the white horses and their riders, following their Lord. Jesus addressed the unbelieving horde, "I AM; I have created everything in the entire universe and beyond that too! I created the tiniest speck of matter to the largest object imaginable. The Triune God, with me at the helm of creation, created life and hold all of life in balance. Today, I pronounce judgment upon you who have rejected me and have even gathered to attack me and my followers. I AM the author and sustainer of life. I removed my grace from you because you have completely rejected me. NOW!" With that pronouncement, the horde and even their horses dropped, for they had no breath, no beating hearts, and no life. With a swishing noise, birds of every size descended upon the flesh, for a feasting like no other.

The angel with the special cord (which was made by Susquehanna, the huge spider of Heaven), brought it to Jesus. He dispatched the angels to gather the demons and Satan; He then bound them and opened the Earth, throwing the screaming, writhing bunch into the abyss. The Earth closed up once again and Jesus and his faithful followers turned away from the carnage and began their walk toward their life back on Earth.

The vision of the valley faded and the people breathed in the fragrance of the bounty before them, almost like they were replacing the memory of the stench with the loveliness that filled the air now. Jesus let that physical response resonate a few moments, then began the teaching, "The Kingdom of God is like this valley. Satan wanted victory over the Divine; what little power he had has been vanquished. Out of the flesh and bones that held evil in every cell, My Power has reigned. I have transformed the negative to be forever beautiful, abundant, and strong. Forever more, this valley will be abundant in flowers of every kind. Regard this highly, for the truth of My Kingdom also is for you. Out of the evil that was once in your lives, there is now beauty, abundance, and strength. Where there once was horrible pain, forever more will be rejoicing."

Applause and praises filled the air, whipping sweet fragrances into tiny turbulent tornados. As the fragrances surged and bounced around, giggles and guffaws erupted. The floral carpet on the hillsides giggled in a twittering of light, fluffy resonances; the children rolling over them seemed to tickle their petals. Sarah mused, "*How remarkable this is, that the flowers are not damaged, but seem to even enjoy the feel of a child rolling over them.*" In a warm confirming and comforting thought, The Spirit of God affirmed as she had discerned.

Jesus lifted His arms high and the jumble of sound calmed. He turned to Sarah and Sally and introduced them, "Sarah and Sally will lead us in an activity, designed especially to affirm the Kingdom of God in each of your lives. Challenge yourself to stretch and participate; not only you will be blessed, but everyone will. Ladies?"

At the moment Jesus lifted his hand to Sarah and Sally, neither had any idea of what it was that they were to do. Sarah rose in complete obedience and faith in their Lord, and as soon as she did, The Spirit gave her the entire idea, almost like an immediate download, right into her noggin! She began, "It is an honor to be with you this beautiful morning. As Jesus shared with us, this morning, His Kingdom is for our own lives. Please consider and share with all of us, how the Kingdom of God is in your life. Just to get things going, Sally and I will go first."

Sarah continued, "The Kingdom of God is ever surprising me! As Jesus spoke, I had no idea what activity we would be doing. Until I stood in obedience and faith, I was wondering what was ahead. It was so fast, I could not conceive of it and yet, I know it would be a huge blessing! The Kingdom of God is a surprise every moment; I love living in the moment of the love of God, learning to appreciate every minute."

As Sarah sat down, Sally arose. She jumped in with a physical leap that startled everyone! As she landed, her words jumped, "The Kingdom of God is a leap with my entire being, physically, emotionally, and spiritually. There is no way to leap halfway! Once I received Jesus as my Savior, I was in all the way. From that time until this very moment, He has taught me to leap with courage, anticipation, and absolute trust in His ability and desire to bless me. It is an exciting life!" With that, Sally queried the gathering, with her eyes meandering over each person, "OK, who would like to share next?"

A gentleman with a humongous belly lifted his hand and grasped the hands 'of people around him, as he gingerly arose. He had a pudgy face and every feature smiled with His joy. He shared, "I'm Connor and I have just recently become a Christian. The Kingdom of God is absolutely newness of life for me. My life was filled with angry outbursts at work, drinking beer every night, and lashing out against those I love so much. Now, there is only joy and sweet love with, and for my family. It is like a beautiful dahlia where there was before a dead, burnt up stub." He exclaimed, "Thank you, Jesus, for renewing my life!"

Jesus stood and replied, with a voice full of compassion, "It is my joy to bless you, Connor." He walked over to Connor, who fell into the Lord's open arms. Sarah was pensive, "*This is indeed the most masculine thing to do, to be refreshed in the arms of the Lord. In Him, there is complete freedom.*"

Sally stood up and two hands shot up; she pointed to one and a young lady who was sporting a jumpsuit with culottes hopped to her feet. She held up a wadded up napkin and proclaimed as she unwrapped it, "My life was being wasted away with MS, Multiple Sclerosis, like a used up paper napkin." She exclaimed, "Jesus changed that!" amid thunderous applause. When she looked again at the wadded-up napkin, it had changed too! She almost burst in her exuberance, "He made me a new creation, a profoundly healthy creation, just like this napkin." She waved the napkin, which had become a silk cloth, with delicately embroidered, metallic thread forming her name, Lorene. The metallic thread caught the sunlight and sparkled for everyone to see. She jumped up and down and ran to Jesus, who caught her up and swung her around and around. When at last He released her, she leaned for a moment against His chest and looked into His eyes and whispered, "Thank you for your love."

Those who rested upon the floral bounty, feasted upon the glory of the Lord. Every person had a unique and powerful witness about the Kingdom of God. As Sally encouraged the other person who had volunteered at the same time as Lorene, several people began to dance and sing their praises to the Lord, not loudly, but beautifully, as if singing a background to the stories of grace and love. The older man stood and introduced himself, "I'm Horace. The Kingdom of God is new for me; I became a Christian as a direct result of the beauty and joy I watched in my wife's life." He squeezed her hand and she stood up as well; he lifted her hand high, amid great applause. He continued, "The Kingdom of God is like a flowing river. His love always flows, never dries up, and covers all the hard places of life. I was once a hard place, mean and gruff; but now, I am soft, and ready to receive the life-giving water of my Savior." He bowed low to Jesus, as he finished.

The praise-laden singing had added base and baritone voices. The singers increased in volume as Jesus walked with compassion toward the bowing gentleman. A gentle embrace, enclosed in honor, held all of creation enthralled. That was the moment Sarah realized that there was more to this than merely an exercise. Angels hovered in a respectful circle above the valley, riveted with not only the words of humanity, but also the awe-inspiring glory of God. The Earth, sky, and everything Sarah could see joined in to honor the Savior, each with a rumble, a reverberation or an echoing resonance. Sarah thought to herself, "*Wow, if I'd experienced this before my resurrection experience, I'd be exhausted by now. What an exquisite thing this is! Instead of being completely worn out, I want more, ever more of the Lord!*"

At length, Sarah stood and asked if anyone else would like to share. A little boy jumped out of his mother's arms and lap and hollered, "I want to!" When Sarah nodded to him, he belted out in his best, biggest voice possible, "I'm

Billy. The Kingdom of God is like the biggest party you ever saw! It never ends! I love parties and I love you, Jesus!"

Jesus did not want to diminish the exuberance of this little guy's love. He leapt into action, running between individuals, scooping up pintsized Billy, swinging him around and around, and showering him with tickling kisses, which garnered riotous giggles! Laughter rippled across the valley; everyone joined the party!

Way across the valley from where Sally and Sarah sat, a young girl's voice floated upon the warm breeze, lifting up praise for the Lord. It was beautiful and sweet, singing the beloved words:

> "Be thou my vision, O Lord of my heart;
> naught be all else to me, save that thou art -
> thou my best thought, by day or by night;
> waking or sleeping, thy presence my light."

The beauty of her voice reverberated throughout the valley and with the next verse, more and more voices joined in her praises, with harmonious voices filling the air:

> "Be thou my wisdom, and thou my true word;
> I ever with thee and thou with me, Lord.
> Thou my great Father; thine own may I be,
> thou in me dwelling and I one with thee."

As the melodious voices continued, they grew in intensity and power. Jesus set down His bundle of love, Billy, and began to walk among those He loved. He hugged tenderly, caressed sweetly, and kissed cheeks and hands passionately. He blessed as He was blessed:

> "Riches I heed not, nor vain, empty praise;
> thou mine inheritance, now and always;
> Thou and Thou only first in my heart,

high King of heaven, my treasure thou art.

High King of heaven, my victory won,
may I reach heaven's joys, O bright heaven's sun!
Heart of my own heart, whatever befall,
still be my vision, O Ruler of all."

Jesus lifted his arms, hands and eyes toward Heaven, declaring in deep baritone melody, while the entire assemblage was held captivated and beloved,

"We give you, Father God,
All the glory for every good thing.
Our fellowship is unity,
One God and yet three unique and blessed individuals,
Our fellowship is wide-ranging;
Our Spirit uniting people and God in absolute joy.
This is the fellowship for which creation happened,
Blessing and being blessed,
Honoring and being honored,
Loving and being loved
Forevermore!"

As Jesus sang, people began to rise and dance with arms outstretched toward Heaven. As more and more arose, Jesus also rose, above the valley, more of worship and His complete abandonment of any other thought, than any interest to lift himself up.

The people were astounded when Father God blessed them, releasing a powerful wave of Divine Love upon them. They were moved, literally, by such a love that no one had ever experienced. They were flattened, while at the same time lifted up, so that they floated on the love of God, at varying distances above the flowery valley. "Thank you" and "Ah" and "Oh" echoed from blessed lips. The anointing had no limits of time; indeed, there was not even a thought of time in all worshipers. Their only thought was resting in this absolute love of God.

At length, Sarah slowly returned to Earth; she humbly looked around and observed this exquisite anointing. She whispered a "Thank you" to the Spirit and immediately received the love again flowing all over her, ever so briefly. She knew if it lasted longer, she would again be floating in its power. She beheld others' joy and release as she sat upon the floral beauty of the glorious valley. Sweet fragrances wafted in; she breathed deep of the beauty - on so many levels.

Presently, there began a flow of light conversations as more people were released from the love wave. Sally came back to Earth and Sarah gave her a moment to gather her thoughts, then said quietly, "Oh my, how the Lord blesses every activity so much more than I would have ever imagined!"

"Wow!" exclaimed Sally, "I agree! There is so much more depth to every activity here, because Jesus is with us, blessing every detail of our gifts to honor Him. He surprises me every day with His love, honor, and glory!"

The gals noticed people were beginning to stand and Jesus had come back to Earth too. Sally and Sarah joined in the walk toward Jerusalem. As the group meandered, people surrounded Jesus, hugging and thanking him, even giggling as he lifted up the children and gave each tickling kisses. Sarah and Sally also made their way toward Jesus and both thanked Him for all His love and blessing. He kissed each on her cheek and thanked them for their willingness to help. Then He told them, "I want you to know, it is because of the unique gifts I placed in you that people are blessed by you guiding these activities." He held them both in a three-way hug and sent an instant wave of love to them, then released them in a lingering hold of their hands. Both stepped back, flushed by His love, and stepped aside to allow others to thank Him too.

As they walked back to Jerusalem, Sarah and Sally talked enthusiastically about the blessings of the day. They could hardly contain themselves, and noticed others all around them were just as animated in their conversations. Sarah thought to herself for a moment and then voiced her perception, "You know, I am realizing that we will not forget these blessings. From that first Resurrection Morning, I am able to remember every activity, perception, and interaction that I've experienced. In fact, I think there's even more to it than that. As I visit with you and others, I am able to add to my own experiences and learn to appreciate every blessing even more!"

Sally replied, with her whole face lighting up as the new realization hit home, "Yes, you are right! This is huge; it expands the blessings that we experience, so that we will continue to learn, receive His love, and be more able to bless others as we grow."

"It is huge!" Sarah agreed. "It is also very exciting, so much more than our struggle when we lived on Earth the first time, trying to remember details of life, but losing them to old age! You know, I bet we can do that review of history, of any occurrence that we would like to refresh our memories about and from that point on, all the details would be a part of our expanded memory capacity."

"I think you're right," agreed Sally. "That would be a good activity for the nights when those who haven't yet had their body-shift are sleeping. It's always quiet at night and I love the peace and beauty of nighttime. By the way, I would love to duck into a little shop and have a passion smoothie! How about you?"

"It sounds good to me!" Sarah quipped, as she opened the door of a quaint café. Sitting down with their cool, fruity-sweet smoothies, the ladies continued their visit. As they yakked, Sarah noticed that many others were also chatting about the day's events. Then, they began talking together, everyone in the café. Each individual shared and listened in rapt communion of receiving such love that they were both brought low and lifted up. It was so fascinating, that before they even noticed the passage of time, dusk signaled the approaching night.

Sally leaned over to Sarah and whispered, "I'm feeling quite overloaded with such a powerful blessing and then all the sharing. I think I'll slip out and rest a bit."

Sarah hugged her friend, whispering in her ear, "Yea, I'm chock-full myself. But it sure has been fun!" They stood slowly, not wanting to interrupt the group dialogue, and quietly waved their "Good-byes" and stepped into the street, enveloped in the descending nightfall. The cool night air refreshed them both; for a moment, they merely stood and breathed deep of its appeal.

Presently, Sally and Sarah both began to talk, at the same time! Then they laughed and Sally said, "Tag, you're it! You go!"

Sarah giggled at her friend's sweet reminder to childhood games. She stood up and jumped in, literally – doing a long jump as she replied, "Well I thought I'd jump in and suggest we pray as we walk back to the house, asking the Spirit what the activity is for tomorrow." Over the seasons, they had continued to assist Jesus with the new believers' groups. It really blessed them to watch believers grow in faith and blossom in their gifting, to the glory of God.

Sally stood and jumped two quick bunny hops, grabbing her friend's hand and saying, "Let's do!" Hand in hand, eyes open so they could see where they were walking, they prayed with Sally leading, "Lord God, we were so very blessed today. We cannot imagine what you may have prepared for tomorrow, but we love serving you and all of your family this way. Please tell us how we may help, to give you honor and glory, for the Name of Jesus to be ever glorified! Amen."

They walked together, in silence, waiting patiently and expectantly for the answer. Their hearts were full of the joy of the day; the beauty of the stars glistening above their heads, so close they could almost touch them. They both heard the Spirit, audibly, as if He were walking next to them, "My dear ones, your willingness blesses me as much as the specific actions you do in service to my beloved. Because I know and cherish my beloved, and I know that this day has been such a great and powerful blessing, tomorrow will be a day of rest and having fun. Enjoy your day tomorrow, for even in the rest, my blessings are abundant! Then, the following day, I have an activity prepared for the children, and I will need your assistance for that."

The gals chimed in together, saying exactly the same thing, even in the same intonation, "Oh, Thank You, Lord!" Then, they giggled like school girls at their identical response. They continued their walk home, chattering on, hand in hand, like they never would let go of their friendship. After a while, they arrived to the point they needed to split, one turning left a few blocks and the other in the opposite direction a few blocks. Sarah grasped her friend with surging emotions, exclaiming the joy of their friendship, "Sally, from the moment we met, God has showered us with blessings we both cherish. I love you so, my dear friend."

Sally hugged her friend fiercely, agreeing with all that was in her, "You are so precious to me! Who could have ever imagined that God would take our humble beginnings in a run-down mobile home park and bless us so much, as well as so may we have the privilege to serve? We are quirky, you and I, and God knew what He was doing when He brought us together in Him!"

With a quick, "He sure did!" Sarah held Sally's hand, then slowly slipped hers away, parting them for a day of rest. She said lightly, "See you the day after tomorrow!"

Sally replied, "See you! Blessings to you…" as she began the short walk to her Earth abode.

"And to you…" Sarah hollered, a bit low-key so she didn't bother anyone nearby. She meandered the last few blocks, absorbing the night beauty into her soul. As she walked, almost drifting home, she lifted her arms in praise of her Lord, who had blessed her so.

Arriving at her Earth home, Sarah prepared a light meal and sank into her comfort lounger to rest and rejuvenate, with food, drink, and the love of God surrounding and soothing her. How she loved to rest in His love!

CHAPTER 7
Rest & Ensuing Intensification

Sarah dined slowly, savoring each bite. She felt the Lord's constant Presence envelop her in such love that she realized that she had never been alone. The Spirit's affirmation directly to her mind allowed her to receive even more healing, which released her from the childhood wounding of her body, mind, and emotions. He said, "I have been with you from the moment you were conceived. My love flowed all around you, blessing you with determination and tenacity, in the face of seemingly overwhelming physical and emotional pain. I helped you when you were little, bringing my love into your life and as you were able, to process the horrible things that were done to you. I have been with you, my love infusing you with compassion, abilities, and power; every moment, every breath has been given to you through my adoring love for you."

Sarah drew in a deep breath, remembering her prayer from so long ago. She whispered, "Abba" and breathed out slowly, whispering, "Father." Over and over, she breathed in – receiving the powerful love of God and breathed out her gratitude. She thought back through her life and like a silent film of her life on Earth, the Lord revealed every detail, every moment and how He surrounded her in His love. She also saw how Keturael ministered the love of God to her. The experience lingered so miraculously, so wonderfully, that Sarah could only receive the revelation of her life and rest in utter awe of her Lord.

After resting from the life review, with the Presence of the Lord in every situation, every good thing and bad, Sarah felt somewhat exposed, like even the most private moments of her life were also quite visible. She asked the Lord about this miniscule aspect of her life in a silent prayer, feeling embarrassed even in the asking.

Sarah heard the compassion-filled response in her ears, but also felt it in her body and somehow, in the center of her emotions. He spoke audibly in His gentle, loving voice, "My dear one, I created you in great and powerful love. I created your body for functionality and to bless you individually and in relationship with others. The intimacy of sexuality in marriage is the highest form of intimacy for humanity and reflects the depth of intimacy possible between the Godhead and humanity. When sin crossed the threshold into the human heart, along with it came embarrassment. I created the human body and the beauty and variety of each individual is a reflection of my love and grace. Parts of the body, or specific actions of the body which seem to be embarrassing are truly blessed in my love. It is very similar to when sin reigned on Earth, how some people who were handicapped or homeless, triggered embarrassment or even a loathing by some individuals and groups of ruffians. In reality, my love for each of them is as profound as my love for you. I look not on the physicality of a person or act, but rather on the covering of love and grace I have placed over them. Does this help, my sweetness?"

Sarah replied audibly, not even thinking first, but bursting forth enthusiastically, "Oh, Yes! I remember being very uncomfortable, before resurrection morning, about intimate moments and bathroom stuff. This really helps me to relax about my body and how you created me for intimacy, and how beautiful that is!"

The night flew by, with Sarah sending queries to the Lord and receiving wise replies from the Spirit. The most profound was His answer to her question of the suffering of her soul when a loved one adamantly rejected Jesus Christ. She had struggled with the deep emotions that rumbled around inside her; to her knowledge, her brother had never even considered a life of faith in Jesus. With her life and body perfected, and sin no longer had a part in her everyday life, she still didn't understand, nor could she put it to rest in her heart and mind. Thinking about the beauty of the love she received from the Lord, she marveled how the pile of outlandish emotions could well up so quickly!

She felt the gentle Spirit show her how much He loved not only her, but also her loved one. His tender words calmed the swirling emotions, "I have loved him from before I even created time itself, as I have loved you. The deepest truth is that only I am able to see into the farthest reaches of a person's thoughts, emotions, and decisions. Your faithfulness to share the truths of my love and grace shone like a guiding flashlight into your brother's anguished soul. He suffered profound agony in life; but under all the pain was a sweet little guy who wanted to be loved. That little fellow (though he was older by human standards, he was young in terms of eternity!) took an ever-so-slight step of faith, as you had indicated for him to consider; it was the beginning of faith in his soul."

As the Spirit of God Spoke to her mind and spirit, Sarah grew more hopeful and more at peace. He affirmed, "Faith begins at the core of a person, at the center of their body, soul, mind, and emotions. Sometimes, the fruit of that faith takes a while to work its way out, toward active parts of a person, their words, actions, and everyday decisions. When there is such extreme pain, as your loved one had suffered, there are walls of self-protection, denial, emotional trauma, and profound loss to break through and defeat. I have been with him, patiently and methodically infusing hope and healing deep within his being. And so it is that he was one of so many, which were hidden from the evil that gripped the world when the antichrist bellowed his worst. In the morning, he will be arriving here from his long journey, from your childhood community. Be blessed, dear Sarah, in this reunion of miracles, with your brother. What Satan meant for evil, The Father, Son, and I have transformed for an eternity of love and healing."

Sarah could hardly contain the joy that flooded her body. She grasped her hands to her chest and gushed, "Oh, Thank you, my Lord and my God! You have blessed me beyond measure! I praise you and thank you!" She jumped up and whirled around and around, arms waiving praises to God and her voice singing boldly of His grace.

When she at long last her exuberance was at least slightly spent, she reclined contentedly and allowed the joy to permeate every cell of her body. She thought, "*Oh, my! The horror and violence that plagued our family no longer has power over any of us. The memory of my own pain is now a blur that hurts now about as much as a poke from a straight pin. How I struggled with the suffering my brother experienced all his life, the physical and emotional trauma gripping him like a vise, hard and strong! I've prayed for so many years, that the comfort and peace of Christ Jesus that I have received and shared with him, would solicit in his heart and soul a sliver of longing for Jesus' love. What blessing is mine, to learn that indeed, my prayer was answered so powerfully! He is coming! I will see him blessed! Oh, my! What joy fills my soul!*"

After resting a bit, soaking in the Father's love, Sarah prepared a sumptuous fare of fruit, vegetables and sweet passion tea. She gathered the munchies onto a tray and slipped out into the waning darkness, to welcome this new day of such promise. Sipping the hot tea, Sarah surveyed the lightening sky, which had streaks of wispy clouds. As she popped her favorite juicy berries into her mouth, the sun popped up over the horizon, glistening in effervescent beauty with the hint of the warmth to come in its wake. Sarah found her excitement level increasing, like the feeling of great anticipation that comes with the first day of a vacation, school, a job, or a wedding day, or even the birth of a child. She felt giddy with expectation; in a silent prayer, she asked the Spirit where she should go to meet her beloved Leroy.

She quickly felt and heard the response in her head, not audibly, but rather the gentle impression of tender words upon her mind, "My dear one, you are so precious! Your brother is walking in his journey, because he is so grateful to no longer have pain in his knees or hips. When he stepped out in faith, even as confused as he was, he longed to be released from the arthritis pain. Oh, how I loved giving him the gift of physical restoration! He is coming from the west, after taking a cruise ship from New York City to Tel-Aviv. If you walk west beginning on this path, (He indicated the walking path nearby) you will meet him. Be blessed, my beloved."

Sarah sprang to her feet and took her tray back into her abode, leaving it on the kitchen counter. She flew out the door and onto the path, then started skipping down the path, reaching higher and father with each hop than she ever could in her youth. She began singing, in her sweet alto voice,

> "Skip, skip, skip to my Lou;
> skip, skip, skip to my Lou;
> skip, skip, skip to my Lou;
> skip to my Lou, my darlin'!"

She felt like she was eating up miles, skipping easily through the neighborhoods to the west of her abode. As the sweet song of her youth ended, Sarah chuckled at the transformation of her body from its arthritis-riddled joints before Resurrection Morning, to her youthful, energetic, and pain-free body that she experienced now. She could feel anticipation well up from deep inside; it was fun, familiar, and full of the joy of receiving God's love.

Chapter 8
Rejoicing Reunification

Sarah gasped, as she rounded a corner and there Leroy was! He was leisurely walking, watching the birds flit from one bush to another, engrossed in their beauty. He had a backpack slung over his shoulder and carried a mug, his ever present love of coffee well evident. She slowed down, to avoid shocking him with a quick approach. She noticed his gait was easier than the last time she had seen him, when his knees buckled with arthritic pain. He glanced her direction, saw her broad smile and opened his arms and said endearingly, "How's my sister, my Sarah?"

Sarah ran the last few steps into his arms, hugging and exclaiming, "Wonderful, and so thankful to see you Leroy!" He swirled her around and around, and she let her legs fly out, just like she did when she was a little tike and he a teenager. They both laughed and hugged fiercely, even when Leroy stopped the twirling.

"Oh, I have so much to tell you!" Leroy said. "So much has happened since I last saw you. Do you know of a little café near here? I'd like to sit down for a bite and visit."

"I sure do!" Sarah replied. "Let's take a right here and we'll see a cute little café." They walked from the trail to a nearby road and only two blocks later, were settling down with croissants, steaming hot coffee, and hot spiced cider in a beautifully decorated floral shop/café. Sarah, drawing in a deep breath of the luscious fragrances, could hardly contain her excitement; she jumped in, "Leroy, will you share with me first about how you received the Lord Jesus? My prayers for you were answered, in the love and grace of our Lord!"

Leroy responded, "Sure, it is an absolute joy." They sipped their coffee and cider, as he continued, "All the pain, anger, and outright hatred left the moment I took a tiny step of faith; it vaporized like the puff of steam it really was! Perhaps I should go back to our last few years before the rapture. Do you remember our talks?" When she nodded, he continued, "I remember my thoughts fixated on how much I hated even the thought of God. I hurt so bad from all the stuff that happened in our youth, that I blamed God for everything that went wrong, everything that hurt, and even things that I, myself had caused because of the way I treated people I wanted so desperately to love. It was so easy to blame God and then, all the personal responsibility of my own actions faded into the background.

Leroy further explained, "In the face of my constant barrage of vitriol against God, you patiently shared how the love and grace of Jesus Christ heals the deep wounds of abuse and trauma. You gave me little snippets of what faith looks like in everyday life. Perhaps you did not realize how our talks were setting a foundation for my salvation, but thank God (he briefly lifted his hands and face toward Heaven) that He used our visits to give me things to chew on. I chomped on the words you shared, often cogitating for days, trying to maintain my anger and hatred. With each visit, my cynical heart softened to the grace and love that you shared; I longed for them both myself. I was tired of the ugliness that oozed around my anger and hatred; I longed, with a yearning deep inside me, to love and be loved. When I finally admitted that fact, I realized that I truly had a choice to make. Did I want to stay with my anger and bitterness against God, or did I want to find out if there could possibly be a God who would fill my life with love, like what I observed in my little sister's life? I'm so thankful that I chose to ask, 'Jesus, if you are real, show me.' That same night, He came to me while I slept and showed me His wounds; when I touched Him, He filled me with His love and healing. When I awakened, I asked Him to come into my life and heal my brokenness. I asked Him, 'Please fill me with love. I am tired of anger and hatred; it has taken too much from me, my family, my friends, and my life. I am trying to take a step of faith. Please help me.' Then I said, 'Amen,' like I've heard at the end of prayers before."

When Leroy stopped for a breath, Sarah grasped his hands in hers and exclaimed, "I am so thankful you chose to seek God and His love and grace! Words cannot express the delight this brings to my heart; this is a huge blessing!"

Leroy smiled immensely and continued his story of faith, "From the moment of my prayer, Jesus healed my brokenness and replaced it with love. The first thing I noticed was the overwhelming sadness was gone. I had struggled for years with depression and loneliness. I had hurt people whom I really did love and when that pain pounced back at me, I was so hurt that I stayed away from relationships. I built walls around myself, to keep people away and insulate myself from further pain; but that triggered great loneliness. My heart and soul was scarred with black ilk that infused anger, fear, and hatred into its ugly grip on me. In the moment of my prayer, Jesus cleaned my deepest pain; without any pain or struggle, He scoured out the damaging bitterness and in its place, He filled me with love. I never knew such joy was even possible! I remember thinking of my pain like my entire body had been attacked with a meat cleaver, deep gashes that oozed blood and pain. Jesus not only healed every gash, but transformed every cell of my body with the balm of His profound love."

Leroy was on-a-roll! He continued, "Do you remember how I used to travel around in my big van?" When she nodded again, he threw up his hands and exclaimed, "I've been traveling differently since Jesus opened my heart to His beauty. Jesus healed my arthritis and gave me strength and stamina again. I feel like I did when I was 20 years old, wow! I've had so much fun, first trekking on foot across America, with only a pack on my back. It took oodles of time, but I sure saw the beauty of the land, the waterfalls, mountains, and oh, the Grand Canyon!

"I didn't realize I'd be coming to Jerusalem, but along my walk, I think in Tennessee, I met a dear lady who offered me a meal and a Bible. She was so gracious to me; I accepted her kindness and received her gifts. It was then that I began to read about Jesus. The more I read, the more everything was confirmed that had happened in my heart. I knew I wanted to live where He lives; I also learned about the Spirit of God and how He is with me, and in me! It took me awhile to get used to the Presence of God being in me, but the more I received His love, the more I rested in His Presence and listened to His guiding voice. When I reached New York City, after a short jaunt upstate to see Niagara Falls, I secured my passage to Jerusalem. On the ship, I heard a lot about battle of Armageddon and the removal of Satan for a thousand years. It was old news by then, but wow, it was great news! I spent most of my time onboard studying Scripture and being mentored by other believers. The cruise took quite a long time; at each port, we took on more passengers heading for the Holy Land. We arrived at Tel-Aviv two days ago. I have loved walking in newness of life and love. With my daily readings of His Word, I am soaking in the power and provision of my God. There is absolutely no way I am able to thank you enough, my dear Sarah. It was your love, persistence, and prayer that God used to get into the hard shell of my brokenness. I will love you forever and then some more!"

Sarah hugged him tenderly, then responded, "I love you, too. You are so precious! The negative was so awful, but now – in the light of this joy we have, it is more like a bad dream. Every moment that we experience living in the fullness of God's love, the past pain fades more and more. When we finish our coffee and cider, I think the first thing we should do is go to see Jesus. He is beyond words, beyond my capacity to even describe; at the same time, He is boundless in love, blessing everyone from the youngest to the oldest."

"That's exactly where I'd like to go!" affirmed Leroy. They both received the confirmation from The Spirit, a wonderful tingling that gushed over their bodies, from top to toe! Leroy sounded a bit lightheaded when he commented, "I love the communication of God; He has so many ways of blessing us!"

"He sure does!" his sister agreed. "I am sensing more and more, how His compassions are new every morning; His love is beyond comprehension. Trying to gather my thoughts around that makes me feel like I'm going to POP!"

"I feel like that a lot, these days," acknowledged Leroy. "I think it's because I'm still new to faith in Jesus. Everything is a bit confusing, in my head. What I can say is this; my heart is clean and new, and is completely released from the overwhelming blight that Satan had me tethered to. So, even if I don't understand completely the details of living a life of faith, I am enormously confident of Jesus' transformation of my life. I remember hearing about childlike faith; I think that's what I have now. I am no longer questioning who and what Jesus is, like when I was a cynical atheist, but now I know, that I know, that He has changed me! I am open to learning more; in fact, I want to soak in everything about my Lord, like a big, thirsty sponge. The Spirit has guided me in my journey here, to see Jesus and live in the epicenter of His life-enhancing teaching. I am anticipating living in His Presence with great enthusiasm. I know I have had the Spirit of God with me and in me. I struggle with reverberating confusion as to how that is even possible, but I am learning, with God, everything is possible! My point is this: His Presence with me and in me; He has greatly blessed me with guidance, peace, and discernment. Yet, I am still seeking, no – yearning for more of Him."

"I agree, absolutely!" exclaimed Sarah. "As much as I thought I've known, I'm learning and yearning for even more of Jesus, every day. The Spirit has taught me that for me to experience Him, I need to be open and seeking Him, willing to abandon all my pre-conceptions, fears, and concerns. I need to be ready to receive Him in any way He chooses to infuse me with His Presence. The process involves all of my senses, emotions, intellect, and all of my body. I am learning to yield thoroughly to His Spirit. One of the most profound ways that I have found to do this is through worshipping the glory and honor of the Triune God. There are wondrous occasions to express worship, especially with the people of God all around and Jesus Himself is with us! Moreover, God blesses us in the midst of that worship. It is exceedingly personal; worship may be expressed when you are reposing in a moment of solitude, or immensely conveyed in the hub of a crowd. I truly believe it is in worship that I have been most intensely blessed than any other time of my life. I often feel waves of love washing over me like ocean waves upon the beach. Sometimes, I'm not sure if I can handle all the blessing; I wonder if my body will just burst! But The Lord knows what I am able to handle and when He releases me from intense blessing, I know it is not because He loves me any less. But rather, it is because He loves me that He releases me, to cherish the moments of such powerful blessing, and to bring me increase – of receptibility and appreciation for all He has given."

"Sarah," Leroy said, his words husky with emotion, "You are showing me, by example, all that I too, will be experiencing in Christ Jesus. I think I need to meet Him ASAP! My longing has heightened with just listening to you. Would you like to go now?"

"Yes, let's go!" Sarah replied, as she stood up, pushed her chair in, and sipped the last of her hot spiced cider. She thought, *"Mmmmm that is so good! "* It's like nothing I've ever had before and I love it!" She watched her brother swallow the last of his coffee and thought, *"I remember praying, but oh, how I hesitated to trust God for her brother's salvation. Now, I can see the clarity of my fear that he would refuse over and over, until the time for choosing was over."*

Sarah sent a silent prayer seeking forgiveness for not having greater faith toward her God, who through the Spirit responded immediately, "Yes, sweet Sarah, we forgive you. It is precious that you recognized the error. The power of God to see deep into the human heart and to reach one who has been so profoundly hurt and bring healing balm, is often beyond human comprehension."

Sarah and Leroy stepped from the cool of the café, to the warming Mediterranean morning. People hustled about, with smiles flashing the joy of the morning and greetings flowing as warm as the weather.

Knowing their destination, the Spirit whispered to the siblings, tickling their ears teasingly as He did so, "We have another blessing for both of you, as you make your way toward Jesus, who is in the Garden of Gethsemane. He loves blessing people there and redeeming the garden from so much torment the night of His betrayal."

They turned slightly and started heading for of the famous garden. They both had confirmation that the direction was accurate, even if the timing may be a bit different than they had anticipated. As they ambled through a marketplace, Leroy marveled at the huge variety of wares available. Money was no longer an issue; hence there was no need to haggle over prices, or worry about people stealing. Every item was for whoever needed it; it was the utopia the siblings had talked about long ago, and longed for. In fact, Leroy's longing was so strong that he had hand-written a book of such a utopian life, filling 27 huge notebooks, back in the day of his rampant atheism.

Leroy remarked, "It is even better than I imagined and wrote about. I know now, it is the love of the Lord which makes it so. Every person is valued; every single person can be trusted and therefore, there is no need for jails, policemen, or those pesky laws that told everyone what the can and cannot do. This is Utopia, life in Christ Jesus!"

"You are unequivocally right!" Sarah declared. "It is such a beautiful life, every person experiences the total value that Jesus gave us when He formed our bodies in secret, in the womb of our mother. I love life here with all believers from all time!"

Leroy merely hummed, "Mmmmmm," because he was transfixed by the view ahead. The marketplace transitioned into a flourish of dancers, flamenco, cloggers, square dancers, and line dancers. Each group captivated audiences of folks, who had been milling about, with splashes of color, movement, and melody. Leroy rubbed his hands together and said with great fanfare, "This is pure joy for me; I so enjoyed dancing the Zillertaler Landler with Mom, so long ago!"

Sarah chuckled, remembering the two of them dancing the beautiful German dance, Leroy in Lederhosen and Mom in a Dirndl. Then, the two siblings were astounded; their mother and father were stepping up to the stage, to offer their performance of Zillertaler Landler! The most striking of all was the fact that their joy, peace, and love shown on their faces. In that moment, the thought of Sarah and Leroy walking to see Jesus flew right out of their heads, like a flock of birds taking flight, fast and furious. Family time was so precious to them both; it took preeminence for the moment. The last time Sarah had seen her parents, they all played cards together, Dad's favorite game – 31. She remembered their weathered faces, burdened with life and pain. When she had gone back to college, during the very next week, her father died in an industrial accident. She remembered her visit with her dad in Heaven and how their relationship had grown, she felt warm all over, blessed by the grace of God, that He brought them all into His kingdom. The two siblings watched, as their parents swirled about, with deft movements and laughter embellishing their dance.

When the dance ended, William and Nancy popped off the stage and sat down at a table, breathing resolutely, like they were just a bit winded. They looked up and were just as amazed, perhaps even more, to see Sarah and especially, Leroy, coming toward them. Their eyes swelled and their faces lit up like a Christmas tree! They jumped to their feet and hugged bigheartedly both their children, like mother and father Teddy Bears. Then, they all sat down to visit, each thanking the Lord God, privately and profusely, that their family was intact in their acceptance of and commitment to the Lord Jesus.

Looking absolutely striking in her Dirndl, Nancy was the picture of health, vitality, and joy, with her thin, fine hair of pre-resurrection life being replaced with thick, flowing brunette tresses that heightened the beauty of her chocolate eyes. William was just as full of vim and vigor as Nancy. Leroy was amazed at his full head of jet-black hair; as long as he could remember, his father was bald, sometimes even shaving his own head. Leroy even remembered his father shaving his youthful hair and he hadn't been too thrilled about it either!

Surprising everyone with her great confidence, which was completely absent in their memories of when they were young, Nancy was the first to ask the most pertinent question, "When was it that you received the Lord, Leroy? Do tell; we are most interested!"

"It was this little gal here," Leroy replied, as he squeezed Sarah's hand playfully. "She was one of the very few who would take time to really talk with me. With every visit, she loved me more and sweetly shared her faith in Jesus; she even challenged my ideas of a utopia without God. Invariably, she pointed out the incongruous ideas I put forth and my great concept of utopian life devoid of the

Creator and how it would ultimately shatter. I often spent hours afterward picking up the shards of ideas that seemed so clear previous to our talk and were splintered by the truth she revealed, truth I could not deny. One day, she suggested a question I could ask and take action on it either way I answered it. If I was right in the assumption that there is no God, then nothing would come of me asking a non-existent God to reveal Himself to me. There would be no consequence, positive or negative. However, if I was wrong in the assumption that there is no God, than asking God to reveal Himself to me, would only result in truth being revealed. Then, I could choose to accept Him or reject Him. After that visit, I chewed on the logic of her suggestion. After ruminating on it for more than a week, I finally chose to ask God to reveal Himself to me. I even told him that I may choose to reject Him.

"Well," Leroy continued, lingering on the word, "I went on to other things, writing more about my idea of Utopia. It wasn't until I slept that I had my answer. In what seemed to me to be more than a dream, perhaps it was a vision, Jesus came and talked with me. He had me touch the wounds that went clean through His hands and feet, and even the laceration in His side. As I touched Him, I felt the healing of my wounds. When I reached toward Him in faith and touched Him, the absolute truth of God cleaned my physical wounds and my distraught heart. When I awakened the next morning, there was no longer any question that God is real; I asked Him to fill me with His love and He did!" Leroy's face reflected his joy. His eyes sparkled and he smiled so broadly that Sarah could not recall how his face looked back in his atheistic days. Leroy filled the brief silence with, "OK, my story's told, how about you, Dad? From the last memories I had, I never expected to see you here! But for that matter, most of my life, I never expected to be here! Tell us about how you came to follow the Lord."

"Sure," William began. "There were so many things I did that hurt people, especially my family. My story is a story of the love and grace of God. I felt that I was foremost of sinners. I have learned that sin is sin; there is no sin more atrocious than another. Humanity tends to put labels on one thing or another, like lying supposedly being less than murder. But in the perspective of Gods judgement of sin and provision for forgiveness, every sin is just as heinous and in need of forgiveness as every other sin. Suffice it to say, I was skilled in sinning. My story began to change about six months before my death. I didn't perceive why at the time, though I know now it was God wooing me; I began to be interested in spiritual things. Actually, it was more than just an interest, though it started mildly enough. Soon, I found myself actively seeking God, reading the Bible and listening to Christian programs on the radio. There is one beautiful passage that describes a person who seeks God will find Him, Acts 17:7. If anybody was seeking God, it was me. I couldn't get enough of the Lord. It was like I was coming out of a huge desert and wanted to drink gallons of grace and love. The more I soaked in Jesus, the thirstier I was! I could not have told you the exact moment I received Jesus as my Savior, but Jesus knew my heart – even when I didn't, and when I arrived in Heaven, He told me! There was a moment in time, when I took a step of faith, personalizing the truth I was learning from the Bible and from other Christians. Somewhere deep inside, I said 'Yes! I want this eternal truth, without it life is only brokenness and pain. Jesus, be my truth, my life, my all!' All I remembered was the switching of a light socket, from **Off** (filled with death, abuse, pain and horror) to **On**, to life in Christ, which fulfilled every need and longing with love, peace, and joy. It is fascinating to me that the Lord knew the timing of that industrial accident, which took my mortal body and smashed it. Excitement about knowing Jesus more swirled deep inside and propelled me heavenward when my body died. What captivates me is that before my death, the changes inside my heart and soul had not yet disseminated into changing my hurtful actions toward others. I think perhaps, I was a bit less domineering or abusive, but the horrible habits I had developed over the years! Habits are horrendous to break. I am so thankful that in Christ, I have learned a new way of life. Now, your mother and I love each other with a more powerful, profound love than we ever had on Earth before, and we're not even having sex!"

With that exclamation, all four burst into laughter. Sarah thought she might fall out of the chair, she was giggling so much! When the laughter finally waned, Nancy began to share, "Well, to change the subject back to our personal stories, I will share mine. When I was a little girl, my mother took me to church, but there was so many demands and such confusion about what to do and what not to do, I became disillusioned with all churches. I liked riding my horse more! Nevertheless, I remember that I wanted to be friends with Jesus, a choice I made when I was very little, perhaps when I was about two years old. I never really grew in my faith because the blunders of so many churches seemed to me to be so rotten; I just felt it was OK to not even bother with them. I realize now that the churches were merely groups of very fallible individuals, so there were bound to be mistakes here and there. It would have been helpful for me to learn more about The Bible. I was so confused that when that horrible fire happened, and our precious Timothy died at the tender age of 9, I just broke. I thought that our first-born son must be sacrificed, like the first-born of Egypt dying, when Pharaoh refused to allow the Hebrews to leave the slavery they had endured for hundreds of years. I had things so terribly mixed up, things of faith, and my broken heart, from the pain of living on Earth and losing the son I loved so much.

"I lived my entire life as a child-in-faith with Jesus. It wasn't until I lived in Heaven, that I began to grow in faith, to understand the fullness of life in the Presence of God. Jesus has brought healing to my heart too; I had been broken and bleeding emotionally throughout my life on Earth, from so many awful things that happened to me. There were good times, to be sure, but my pain outweighed the fun memories, forcing me into deeper confusion and despair. I am so thankful to have that over with! Now, I am be able to dance with two of my special guys, William and Leroy!" With that, she stood up and linked arms with both of the fellas and began to dance a jig. As the fellas whirled Nancy around, they all laughed.

They danced and laughed, then halted abruptly; all at the same moment, they saw Timothy walking toward them from the marketplace; surprise and delight spread over their faces. Leroy was flooded with joy as he hugged his brother, who was just a bit bigger than the last time they played together, the night before the fire that took his life. They bear-hugged for a long time, brothers reunited.

After hugging Timothy snugly, Sarah sat down and leaned back in the comfy deck chair, marveling at the beauty of what was taking place. What began as a short journey to the Garden of Gethsemane with her brother mushroomed into a family reunion, with dancing, hugging and lots of laughter. She adored being in the center of God's will; everything is a blessing and every person is precious. Family is more important than ever before; but even more profound is the absolute, complete family of God. Every man and boy is her brother and every woman and girl, her sister. She pondered the differences of her emotions toward her family of origin and the broader family of God; Sarah found it difficult to describe, even to herself, how the jumble of emotions overlapped and intertwined.

As Sarah contemplated, The Spirit of God gently comforted her; she could feel His tenderness, wrapping love around her body like a warm, soft blanket. He whispered, "It is precious that you desire to understand and describe your emotions concerning all the blessings and relationships within the family of God. It is often beyond the human capacity to delineate all the intricacies of relationships. We created you to essentially be 'in relationship' with each other and with us, Father, Son and Spirit. Relax and allow the emotions to flow, accepting each one at the moment and exploring the depth and power of that emotion as you are able to devote more time to the effort. Eternal life is exciting, in that there is always more time."

Sarah breathed deep, to receive everything the Spirit had encouraged her to discern. So much of her maturing process in Christ has been learning to relax and allow God to work His blessings and encouragements in every situation, every relationship. She soaked in the beauty of the moment, cherishing the continuation of relationships that ooze true, selfless love and are devoid of the pain that once monopolized their lives.

Upon the urging of his parents, Timothy shared his story of faith. "I remember learning about Jesus in the little church we visited when I was young. I remember the story of Zacchaeus most of all. He was the guy that was short like me; yet he wanted to see Jesus. He came up with a great idea of climbing a tree – then he was higher than everyone! Jesus saw him up there and knew his heart of faith and He called him down and ate dinner with him that night. When I learned about Zacchaeus, I decided right then and there that I wanted to meet Jesus. The teacher said I could do that easily enough. All I needed to do was to ask Him to be my Lord and Savior. Without telling anyone, I did it! From that moment on, my life changed. I didn't want to fight with my little brother, or even bug him so much; I loved playing with him. I also could feel the Presence of the Spirit inside me, helping me to grow in faith and also in my everyday life. I didn't want to steal things with the guys at school, or hurt the girls at recess.

Timothy continued, "I didn't know I would be with Jesus so fast! When the fire happened, I was confused and thought I knew the way to get out. I pulled away from your hand, Mama; I know I shouldn't have, but once I ran the opposite way you were going, I couldn't get back to you. I couldn't see anything and the smoke made it hard to breath. It made my throat hurt and I got under the table in the kitchen. At first, it was easier to breathe, but then it got worse and worse. Finally I let go and cried in my heart and mind to Jesus; He was the only one who knew where I was right then. He must have sent my angel fast because it was only a moment later that Matanel brought me to Jesus. As soon as I was away from that body, which was all full of smoke, I breathed deep of new life and wow, did I feel good! Jesus held me close and told me how much He loved me; I've been having fun with the Lord ever since! It's great to see all of you. I love coming back to Earth, enjoying its beauty and yet, not feeling any pain, like skinned knees or nettle stings!"

Laughter rolled along the table like a bunch of tiny bouncing balls. Sarah thought deep, profound things amid the merriment. *"This is what life was meant to be, unity with our God and with each other. How precious is this grace! We would never have appreciated it so much without knowing the depravity of sin."*

Confirming of her musings, William commented, "This is what family is meant to be, fun, affirming, and loving!"

Leroy suggested, "Sarah and I were just beginning our hike over to the Garden of Gethsemane, to see Jesus. Would you like to join us?" With "Yes's" all around, they began to rise. However, the Spirit slowed them just a bit, with the tender press upon their thoughts. Leroy voiced their response, "Ah, yes. Jesus is here. Our delay was not a delay after all!"

As Sarah enjoyed the day with family, Sally was having a hilarious time with some children. She had taken a walk that turned into a full-out run and came upon a whole bunch of kids playing together in a beautiful park. They all were having so much fun because there was no longer any antagonism between them, but instead love guided their interactions. After introducing herself, and getting to know them a bit, the whole group gathered around her, hungry for teaching about Jesus. They were so enthusiastic when she agreed to teach them a bit that they began jumping and giving her so many hugs, she almost fell down!

After some of the exuberance waned a bit, one of the youngsters piped up with a question, "Sally, would you teach us, maybe, uh, like how to pray?"

Sally responded, "Sure, I can do that. In fact, I have an activity that you might get a kick out of, to help you remember how Jesus taught us to pray. Each step is extraordinary and has been a huge foundation of prayer for generations. I will go through the prayer for you and then we can do this fun activity to remember it.

Sally began with, "For this first time, I just want you to listen to the prayer. So bow your heads, close your eyes, and tune in to praying this as I say the words:

'Our Father, who is in Heaven,
Hallowed be Your Name.
Your Kingdom come,
Your will be done,
On Earth,
As it is in Heaven.

Give us this day
Our daily bread
And forgive us our trespasses,
As we forgive those who trespass against us.
Lead us not into temptation,
But deliver us from evil,
For yours is the Kingdom,
And the Power,
And the Glory,
Forever!
Amen.'

Sally asked if there were any questions about the prayer and some of the kids were confused about what "trespasses" meant. She encouraged them all to sit on the grass and explained, "A trespass is when one person does something that hurts another person. Even though we have received Jesus and have His love in your hearts, sometimes we make choices that hurts another person's feelings. We need to forgive each other, as Jesus forgives us. With this prayer as a foundation for life in the love and grace of God, you will be able to live a life of peace and joy. Are there any more questions?" All of the kids shook their heads no, some of them goofing around – shaking their heads hard to make their hair fly all over.

Sally decided to tell the children about the activity before jumping into doing it. She introduced it with a short question, "Do you remember playing a silly game called 'Duck, Duck, Goose'?" She got a lot of hollers, "Yea, we do!" and "Sure, it was OK." She followed up, "This is based on that game, but with a few changes. First off, everybody stand up in a big circle." When they all got in a circle, she continued, "As we say the prayer, I will tap each person on the head for each word. When we say the last word of each phrase, I will tap the person on the shoulder. That person gets a hug from me and goes and sits down.

It's not a punishment at all; in fact, everyone sitting down can watch the fun, as the circle gets smaller and smaller. We go through the prayer over and over, until there is only one person standing. It helps to have everyone saying the prayer together as we go through the game and that's how you learn the prayer easier! So, do you want to try it?"

The kids jumped up and down, yelling, "Yes," "You bet!" and "Let's go for it!"

"Okey-dokey," Sally began the prayer, tapping each kid's head with each word and with the last word, the shoulder. "Our Father, who is in Heaven." With the shoulder tap, she stepped back and received the hug from the first child, who then stepped back out of the circle and sat down. As the game progressed and the circle got smaller and smaller, Sally found herself getting a bit dizzy. The kids loved the game. The older ones held the younger ones on their laps as they waited patiently for the circle and game to finish. When the last one hugged Sally, everyone hollered, "Cool!" "We made it!"

With about 50 kids in the group, in the course of the game, they went through the prayer quite a few times. They surprised Sally by wanting to do it all over again! They all had such a fun time that one of the kids asked if they could show Jesus and their parents how much fun they were having learning about prayer.

Sally suggested they all sit down a pray about it and listen for how the Spirit would guide them. They all sat down and bowed their heads, opening their hearts as Sally led them in prayer. "Father God, we have had so much fun today learning about this great way to pray. We want to share it with the parents of these great kids, but also with Jesus and anyone else who would be blessed. Would you guide us and show us how?"

The Spirit spoke audibly, in the beautiful baritone voice, for the children to hear and experience His wisdom and grace personally and together. "Each one of you is precious;

we have been honored by your game and your longing to learn about a life of faith. Of course, we would love to have you share this newfound game of faith; how about this evening?"

The kid's jumped up and yelled, "Yah!" almost simultaneously.

"You guys sure do have vivacious energy!" replied the Spirit, with a laughter-tinged voice. Let's meet at the Jerusalem Theater in a couple of hours. Jesus will be there to join you."

A bunch of voices raised up, with arms a-flyin', "Whoop-whoop!" and "You bet!" and another, "Thank you, Lord!" They all started jumping around, doing cartwheels, backflips, and some danced all over the park. Sally joined in the hilarity, laughing as she danced for joy in her Lord.

Meanwhile, Sarah and her family had concluded their stories of each coming to faith in Jesus. They began to glance around, for in their enthusiasm of listening to each other, they had not even noticed others around them. It only took a moment to see their Savior approaching. They all jumped up and surrounded Him, as everyone else had been doing as He walked. His arms were reaching, touching, ever giving love to His people. Jesus took time for each person, loving each in a unique, compelling way. Sarah felt total fulfillment in His Presence; it flowed over her like sweet honey on a donut. In the briefest of moments, she felt a shift happening. It was almost as if something had been out of place and with the slightest move of Jesus' grace and love, it settled into place. It felt to her like that last piece of a jigsaw puzzle brought completion as it was positioned in its proper place.

Furthermore, it felt like a body shift, from the tiniest of cells somewhere deep inside finally coming into fruition.

Jesus affirmed her and the discernment of the shifting part. She could feel it, but could not really identify what it was. He knew questions were popping in her mind like popping corn in hot butter. He merely said, "Walk with me, my dear ones, and I will open your hearts and minds."

Sarah could hardly breathe, as she began to follow His lead, mulling over in her mind what was happening. She could not even slow down her musings. As she looked at her father, mother, and two of her four brothers, Sarah could see the confusion in their faces as well.

Very quickly, the Spirit confirmed to her, "What you are experiencing is real; we have prepared something that will bless each one of you and fulfill your lives in a deeper and more profound way. It will also be an expression of His love for all of humanity." Sarah felt an excitement build with every step she took. She glanced back and forth from Jesus, to each of her family members and hardly noticed where it was that they were going. Surprises are fun, but a surprise from Jesus, Wow! Often, with Jesus, a surprise is life-changing!

Chapter 9
A Stroll with Jesus

Sarah observed Leroy, as he matched Jesus stride while asking Him one of the copious questions that bounced around in his head. Jesus good-naturedly responded in detail. She noted that their discussion just then centered on the idea of each individual's level of choice. Leroy queried how could a person really have free choice to do anything they wanted, while the Father, Jesus, and the Spirit knew already what that choice would be. Sarah remembered the mental wrangling Leroy and her had gone through with that question, back in the time of his self-induced atheism. Often, it seemed like her head would turn to mush after such brain-twisting mental gymnastics.

Jesus gently guided Leroy through the very profound answer, "Yes, this has been a conundrum for people throughout history. Imagine for a moment, that you have prepared for your son an ant farm, one of those skinny aquarium-like containers in which a person is able to see the progression of the ant farm from both sides. When the tiny little ants are placed in the bottom of the tank, with all of the other things they use for their homes, you know – the dirt, twigs, and pebbles, they each have a myriad of choices. As a human, you are able to see how the choices of each affect not only that ant, but also the community of ants. You are not choosing for them, but you are aware of their choices. You are also able to place items in their paths that will assist them, or block any progress that would be detrimental to them over time. With humanity, it is a bit similar, but with much more complexity. The tri-unity of the Father, myself, and the Spirit is so completely expressed in love that humanity has in a sense, a covering for all of the individual choices, whether they are positive or negative. It is called *grace* and even though we know what the choices are, this grace allows for the ultimate best for each individual. At times, we make an adjustment, especially in those who are listening for our voice through the Spirit, but also through other means which are somewhat beyond the scope of human understanding.

Jesus expounded, "It is so very difficult for humanity to perceive how tragedy can bring about something good. Our perspective is beyond human capacity. We are able to view the totality of one's life, all at the same time. Therefore, we are able to view how suffering is able to bring strength, compassion, and a commitment to righteousness to one's life. Therefore, we know the ultimate purpose of suffering before it even begins. If there were no suffering, the profound empathy of caregivers would have never developed. There would be no reason for rejoicing because of healing, for there would be nothing to heal from. Another way to think about this is the choice of relationship. If we, as the triune God, one in Spirit and Truth, forced humanity to be in relationship with us, what type of relationship would that be? There would be very little to rejoice, for humanity would know nothing of the alternative, not choosing relationship with the living God. We much more prefer a joyful relationship which is forged by love, grace, and choice; we all rejoice together and unite in a more complete relationship than would ever be possible without choice. Does this help with your question, Leroy?"

"Oh yes," he responded. "As you spoke I could feel the Spirit imprinting upon my soul the deep truth of your words. It felt like my whole body clicked into a place of complete understanding in an area of my life that has been the most perplexing of my whole life! It was like a misplaced Lego in the building of my soul was restored to its proper place and I could rest!"

At that, everyone laughed, his dad and brother patted him on the back, uttering, "Yo!" and "Glad to hear it, bro!"

Jesus gestured toward a quite café and spoke in the strong, loving, baritone voice that Sarah had come to love, "Would you like to eat with me? I love spending time with you, just visiting together."

They were all touched by the genuineness of Jesus' words. There were no underlying pretenses, or hidden agendas; with Jesus, there was only grace, love, and peace, all in great abundance. They all chimed in, "Sure!" Sarah pondered, as they walked in and sat down, of the blessings of this time with Jesus. She knew in Jesus' presence, abundant blessing flows. Anticipation built, slowly at first, but it kept welling up in her soul, like a spring being wound-up tight. At some point, this spring of-the-blessing-of-the-Lord would be released and it would surprise them all with its power and provision.

After they had each ordered from the sumptuous cuisine offered, Jesus blessed each one, beginning on His left, "William, I infuse you with the wisdom you have been seeking. You will be a resource for young Christians, about living a life of faith and truth." Jesus placed his hands upon William's head and shoulder and breathed upon Him. Sarah could see the blessing pour into William and the effect of it. He could only rest in the power of the Lord; his head lay on the table, with his hands touching his head lightly. He lay that way for quite a while. Everyone waited with the patience of being with the Lord. Sarah remembered her longing to be with Jesus before Resurrection Morning; she fully embraced the preciousness of this communion with her Lord.

Sarah observed her father; gradually, the spiritual dimension of his blessing came into view. She perceived the totality of her father's blessing. It washed and cleansed his thought processes and created new pathways of thinking. Everything was the same and yet, he was profoundly changed. He was still her father and yet, he was made new. The neural pathways of his mind were enhanced by the wisdom of God. While he seemed to be merely resting his head, in reality, he was receiving Divine wisdom.

When William lifted his head, he was renewed, in Jesus' love and grace transformed to be more than he had been. Sarah pondered, *"This is what living in the Presence of God is, being renewed and imbued with power and love."* In great humility, William expressed his gratitude, "Jesus, I honor you because you are the foundation of all life and wisdom. I will always cherish this gift, thank you so much." He bowed his head in honor of all that Jesus is, holy, compassionate, and full of love and grace. As he lifted his head one again, Jesus acknowledged his thanksgiving with a robust hand shake.

Jesus then reached out his hands to Nancy, who placed her hands into His loving grasp. He said to her, "Nancy, I infuse into your body the peace you have sought all your life. My peace is not the absence of conflict, but rather confidence of my love and grace, in the midst of whatever is happening around you. My peace comforts, secures, and protects. With my peace, you are a woman of profound compassion; you will have the confidence of my love to bless everyone with whom you meet. Be blessed!" His breath washed over Nancy and she melted in its blessing.

Sarah watched, enraptured by the glory of the Lord. He had imparted to Nancy His Divine Peace. It seemed to overwhelm her, not physically, but rather in the way the spiritual dimension subjugated the physical. Sarah noticed that Jesus' peace transformed every cell of her body like kernels of rice absorbing water. Nancy breathed deeper of this peace, joy enveloping her like sweet nectar flowing from a flower into a humming-bird's beak. Sarah loved seeing her mother so blessed; it was stunning!

When Nancy unfolded her body and rose from her blessing, she stood and walked around the table to Jesus and hugged Him, and was blessed all over again. At length, she let go of her Lord and kneeled before Him, praising Him. She then went back and sat down. Just then, the waitress brought their meal. The family and their Lord held hands and He prayed, "Father God, we thank you for your provision for this food. In your love, bless the hands who prepared it, brought it to us, and bless our bodies as we eat. We all love you and honor you. In our love, Father, Son, and Spirit, Amen."

They all joined in, saying, "Amen" with more meaning than they had ever before. Sarah's lunch tasted like morsels from the work of a master chef. It was a basmati rice dish, combined with mushrooms, cheese, and asparagus. It was complimented with a delicious fruit bowl, pomegranate, mangos, and watermelon, with sweet yogurt delighting her palate.

William eradicated his hunger with his favorite, roast and potatoes, with gravy covering every crevice, and a cinnamon-pumpkin custard that fulfilled his appetite. Nancy munched on a shepherd's pie, following it with chunky, spiced applesauce. Leroy dove into a platter of delicious seafood, complimented by seasoned potato rounds and a luscious chocolate cake. Timothy crunched into his favorite, a small pizza with the works; it seemed to overflow every bite and he loved it! Jesus ate Lahmacun, which were round, thin pieces of dough topped with minced beef and vegetables and herbs, including onions, tomatoes and parsley, then baked into deliciousness.

They visited in-between bites; Sarah cherished this personal, intimate time with Jesus. She loved that He made Himself totally available, rather than holding himself apart from His people, like some cold king in a castle. Jesus is unequivocally a part of humanity. He humbles Himself to be one of humankind, and to be fully committed to those who have invited Him to be in relationship with them.

As they finished, Jesus gathered their plates and as a servant, took them to the door of the kitchen. His love is a new way of life for all of humanity; He modeled what it is to love - for them to receive and learn. He came back to the table and sat down, then reached across the table to Leroy. Jesus' face radiated compassion, which filled the room, but intensified all over Leroy. Jesus words filled every need in Leroy's soul, "Leroy, I have loved you from before there was even time or an Earth to measure. You are precious to me, for who you are and for your yearning heart and gentle spirit. I give to you today the fullest measure of assurance that you are loved." Then Jesus breathed His blessing upon Leroy; Sarah marveled at his response. Her brother leaned backward, his body draping over his chair, fully engulfed in Jesus' blessing. Sarah began to realize how this day of blessing would transform each of their lives; anticipation continued to build in her spirit.

Sarah merely glanced at Leroy and the spiritual view of his blessing arose. Jesus had blessed him with assurance that he was loved. Immediately, she thought of the beautiful hymn,

"Blessed assurance, Jesus is mine!
Oh, what a foretaste of glory divine!
Heir of salvation, purchase of God,
Born of His Spirit, washed in His blood."

Sarah had seen the Spirit cover Leroy's body in His white-hot love. It was so intense that it seemed to permeate his entire body, but with even more intensity, his head. Sarah remembered the verse in Romans, "the mind which is governed by the Spirit is life and peace."

After quite a while, Leroy lifted his head and reached over to thank Jesus, "You are so gracious and loving, Jesus. My, how you have blessed me today! Thank you, thank you!" And he bowed to the Majesty on High, who was here with them, not some being far away, but here – blessing each of them.

Jesus reached out for Timothy, who placed his hand in his Lord's. Jesus lauded him, "You have a heart so committed to my working in you and through you that you have often forgotten about how precious you are to me. I place in you the strength of a mighty man of valor, as men of old on Earth. You are a leader among my people, blessed and consecrated with power."

Timothy's response to this exhilarating blessing was in and of itself quite surprising. Physically, he was a youngster, as he had chosen to stay a child and grow after reuniting with his parents in Heaven. He simply slid out of his seat, as though he was a raw egg, and slumped into a ball upon the floor. Sarah and the rest of the family were shocked to see his body change before their eyes! He gained in stature and in weight, his muscles bulging below the light shirt and shorts he wore. As his body grew physically, quite beyond their perusal was the change that occurred in his spirit.

Timothy's enormous physical response to the Lord's blessing brought Sarah's spiritual observations to the surface. Sarah had a sense of what was happening because she had asked the Lord in her spirit as they had begun their walk with Him, that He would open her to the spiritual dimension of their visit with Him. It was spectacular to know and feel all the splendor of the spiritual, emotional, and physical dimensions of the blessings they were experiencing. Sarah had learned to love this spiritual discernment, for it blessed her even more than the physical. There was much more depth to every moment lived in the Presence of God, than what she remembered from before this gift had been given to her. It was like the difference between one dimensional and three dimensional thinking; like thinking about the temperature in a room in terms of hot or cold, as opposed to understanding that each person may consider the temperature in a room in terms of their own body's metabolism and response. She was already so familiar with the spiritual dimension that she took it all in without thinking about the process of observing it. Sarah realized that she had had been pondering these aspects a bit and had missed a moment in the physical!

Timothy had stood up and was in the process of sitting down at the table. The response of the family and others all around was visceral; gasps and exclamations of "Wow!" escaped from everyone in the restaurant. Timothy had grown physically, in moments, from a youngster to a very strong man, fully matured. He looked at his hands, arms and legs, marveling that the spindly things that he lumbered around in that very morning were filled out with strong muscles. He was instilled with confidence, understanding and compassion, for all of these are essential in true leadership of faith. Timothy went over to Jesus and knelt on one knee, struggling in the emotion of the moment to muster up a deeply voiced, "I thank you; I honor you, my Lord Jesus." Jesus rumpled his hair and gave him a rough hug, as they both rose. Timothy looked at himself, catching his reflection in a wall mirror, then at Jesus, who was merely an inch or so taller. He lifted his hand for a High 5, which Jesus responded to with His High 5, both bellowing "Yea!"

Sarah watched her brothers now, as Leroy and Timothy guffawed back and forth. Both had a heightened spiritual quality, which had been miniscule before these most marvelous blessings and now blazed in the power of Jesus' love.

Sarah released her spiritual musings and her gaze happened upon Jesus. He reached his hands to her; she place her hands in His and felt his love covering her. She did not have time to fully absorb His love; she would be absorbing it throughout eternity, but oh, how she felt loved! His deep baritone voice declared His blessing over her, "My dear, sweet Sarah, you have been courageous in your pursuit of my love and grace. You have been willing to bare the worst of your pain, to offer others who have been hurting, the comfort, healing, and joy I've given you. I give you now, a renewal of voice, abounding with compassion, love and power. You have been faithful; I will bless you with more, more of all you need, more of all you desire, and more of all my love. I cherish you, my beloved."

Sarah felt as though her whole body was more alive than ever before. She felt tingling, whirling sensations all over her body. She felt in every cell of her body the ambiance of Divine love; she instinctively knew she could not describe it, yet wanted to tell everyone of such love. As she released her body to take all of Jesus' blessing in, she felt the control of the physical diminishing. She first slumped over, then slid down toward the floor and onto her back. She felt her arms and legs fall haphazardly, but had no interest in pulling herself together physically. She wanted to rest in this love, to rejoice in it, for she knew it was for especially for her. After a while, as she became accustomed to this renewed glory within her, Sarah regained herself and climbed up to sit at the table once again. Everyone smiled and laughed together; they all knew how she was feeling. Jesus joined in the raucous, just because laughing was so much fun!

Presently, Jesus spoke of His enjoyment of the afternoon, "Perhaps it is a little off the wall, but I want you to know how much I have been blessed to be with you. It is for this purpose that The Father, The Spirit, and I have created humanity. Our love is all-encompassing; we are blessed to be with you, sharing our love with you and our blessing over you. We are in relationship, family rejoicing together, blessing each other. I am honored and blessed to be with you, rejoicing with you. Life is so precious when we are together; I treasure being with you. I do have one thing I would like to ask you. Would you be interested in attending with me a fun activity that Sally has been preparing with the children?"

Amid gasps of excitement, and affirmations all around, Jesus stood up, hugged each one and led the way to the Jerusalem Theater. Sarah laughed as she jogged just to keep up, for Jesus walked quickly and with purpose. Amid the pounding of her jovial jogging, she pondered the beauty of their visit with Jesus, *"I know now that it was not a visit to talk, but to bless. Jesus is ever blessing those He loves. I will cherish this day of blessing!"*

Soon, Sarah and her family were surrounded by more and more people following Jesus. With each block they traversed, Jesus called out, inviting everyone to come to the children's presentation. Sarah thought it seemed like a sea of heads bobbing, as the throng rapidly progressed toward the theater. There was anticipation in the air, palpable and contagious.

Chapter 10
Children's Blessing

The theater filled fast. Sarah caught a glimpse, from her comfortable seat inside, of men and older boys scrambling to set more seats outside in large rows surrounding the remote theater screens that they had rolled out from the secure hiding places in all eight walls of the octagonal structure. Sarah had seen those screens, huge but hidden until needed, the week after arriving in Jerusalem after Jesus' display of power and grace at Armageddon. She knew everyone would be able to watch and behold the blessings of the children's presentation.

Presently, the lights in the theater dimmed and Jesus stood to introduce the evenings' festivities. He proclaimed, "Tonight is a night of joy. These children are precious!" At that moment, the children all gathered around Him, hugging Him and cheering. When at last they quieted, He continued, "These little ones have prepared a delightful activity that they want you to see. It has blessed each of them and they want you to be blessed, even as they are again. Sally has graciously worked with them. Let's all give her a round of applause for her generous gift of time and energy!"

The applause seemed so loud it would lift the roof right off! The applause outside made the walls reverberate with competing volume inside and out! Sally gingerly walked toward Jesus and motioned for the children to move to their places. They spread out in a huge circle. Jesus sat at the edge of the stage, in a royal velvet-laden armchair. When everyone was in place and quieted, Sally stepped to the front of the stage and introduced the activity. Sarah knew she was working hard to speak clearly and project as well as she could. She did quite well projecting her voice to the huge audience, "We have learned that learning itself will not end, but will continue to build, because we are living in community with the Creator of all things.

Continuing, Sally added, "I began this activity as a fun way to practice and learn the Lord's Prayer. It is an expansion of the fun children's game, "Duck, Duck, Goose!" As you begin to see how this goes, feel free to join in. At that, she approached the children and began the Lord's Prayer, with all the children in unison. She tapped one child's head as they said each word of the prayer. As the last word of each phrase was pronounced, she instead tapped the child's shoulder, whereupon each child whose head wass tapped slipped out of the circle, skipped over to Jesus, received a big hug and a blessing, and sat down on the edge of the stage. They went round and round, with "Our Father", "who art in Heaven", "Hallowed be thy Name," each child saying the beautiful prayer, slipping out of the circle and being thoroughly blessed by their Lord Jesus. With each reciting, which went on and on because there were so many children, the circle decreased by one, at the end of each phrase. "Your Kingdom come", "Your will be done", "on Earth, as it is in Heaven." "Give us today", "our daily bread," Sally kept going round and round, tapping shoulders and heads, as children, parents, and everyone lifted up the prayer of commitment to the Father in Heaven. Children were blessed, by the words of the profound prayer, by the sheer joy of the game, and by the love of God.

As the large group of children in the circle dwindled, with each recitation of The Lord's Prayer, the blessings flowed freely. A new generation of God-followers were receiving the foundation of living in faith, committing Scripture to memory, "and forgive us our debts", "as we forgive those our debtors." "And lead us not into temptation", "but deliver us from evil."

With the last phrases of the prayer and the last two children receiving their blessings from Jesus, the audiences both indoors and outdoors leapt to their feet and applauded in a thundering "Thank You". The children jumped up and down, surrounding Jesus and calling out His name. Sarah laughed at their unbridled exuberance, "We love you, Jesus!" and "Lord Jesus, we honor you!" Sally clasped her hands together and held them below her chin. Overcome by the joy that such a simple activity would inspire, she simply stepped back toward the edge of the stage in awe of Jesus. Each activity she and Sarah were a part of impelled everyone to more and more joy, giving honor and glory to Jesus. Sarah was also in awe; she observed the children experiencing the Lord's Prayer in such a powerful way and how God used her dear friend to bless so many. She marveled that Jesus' love extends to every person, without prerequisite or limit!

After lengthy applause for the children, the men and women of the Lord's Chorus stepped forward from wherever they were, sprinkled throughout the indoor and outdoor audience, humming a gorgeous hymn. They began to sing the most beautiful rendition of the Lord's Prayer Sarah had ever heard. The children gasped, ooooh'd, and aaaah'd because they recognized the very words they had said. The voices were so lovely, Sarah thought they had even merged to be only one voice, yet with the gorgeous variety of tone, depth, and resonance. She found herself fascinated with the beauty and yet, let all the thoughts go and just became part of the music, swaying lightly to the melodious joy of the prayer she had learned as a youngster herself.

When the Lord's Chorus finally let go of the last note, they quietly went back to merely humming the beautiful tune and slowly filed out. The entire assemblage, both indoors and outdoors, felt the precious moment of worship linger in their midst. The children began to filter through the audience, receiving hugs aplenty; then, small groups sauntered out into the Mediterranean evening of warm breezes flowing like a whisper, with the hint of a cooler evening approaching.

Sarah met up with Sally just as they exited the door. Sarah hugged her precious friend and sister in the Lord with great enthusiasm, so much so that Sally had to say, "Whoa down, don't squish me!" and they both giggled as Sarah let go.

Sarah wouldn't let go of Sally's hand though. She swung her hand way up in the front, even as she grasped Sally's, then way in the back, swinging back and forth as she said, "Oh how wonderful you are, to open God's Word to the children in such a beautiful way! My how all of God's people were blessed! When I could steal my eyes away from the circle of children reciting the prayer, I saw all around me men and women captivated by the beauty of an activity which blessed the children in so many ways! It blesses anyone to learn Scripture, for it is indeed, our food and our provision. The game blessed the children immensely; kids absolutely love to play! When they can play and learn of the Lord, wow, it's precious! And the hugs from Jesus; He blessed each child as He hugged them. That is the pouring out of our God to these little ones. I can hardly contain how blessed we all were. I praise God for your creativity and compassion for these precious little ones. Thank you, Sally, for all you have done this evening!"

Sally seemed to be breathless and could hardly choke out, "I'm blown away! What began with a simple children's game transformed into such a powerful blessing for us all! I'm learning more and more, with Jesus' with us, everything of life is enhanced from what we used to call mundane. Nothing is mundane anymore; life has more color, more beauty, more depth of purpose, and more joy with Jesus. Life is so very good with Him. I love doing anything for anyone in the precious Name of Jesus!"

"Me too, my friend," Sarah responded. Then, quick-as-a-wink, Sally was surrounded by first, the children, and after that, the adults. They all were chanting her name and a couple of big, brawny guys lifted her up and carried her to Jesus, who had exited the theater soon after Sarah and Sally. They wouldn't let her down, but two other big fellas hoisted Jesus up onto their shoulders and there begun a procession toward the Temple. A toddler hollered up to Sally if she would start a song they could sing and she thought for only a moment, the began the beautiful children's song of renown, "Jesus Loves Me". In only a moment, voices from all around lifted up this truth, echoing the sweet refrain, "Yes, Jesus loves me; the Bible tells me so."

The procession came to the Temple already in worship of Jesus. Sally was gently released, whereupon she merely knelt before Her Lord. In a rippling of bodies, the entire populace followed her example, not out of a sense of duty, or to belong to the group, but with true, honest, deeply heart-felt worship. God was among them; their joy of life flowed like a flood, overcoming even the tiniest of little tikes. Children were most precious in their expression of love and worship, dancing before Jesus, then running up to Him and laying down at His feet, wrapping their little bodies around his feet, legs, and even pulling on His arm in fun. He knew their love and they knew His.

Sarah rose from her prostrate position to sitting on her haunches. She watched with wonder how every individual was experiencing this worship differently. She felt herself swooning with the heady waves of love that continued to wash over the people of God. The children frolicked in it; some of the women danced, even in synchrony with each other. The men began to sing their worship, enhancing the fervor of praise. Jesus merely reached out to the people whom He loved and waves of blessing whirled into their joy, increasing it exponentially. Finally, there came a moment that Sarah felt that she could not experience even a moment more of Jesus' powerful pouring out of His love. It was almost like she was stretching out like a huge, thick balloon and right then, she thought she might "pop!" As soon as she thought it, she was back in her Earth abode.

Taken aback by the abrupt shift, for she had not perceived thought travel possible back on Earth, Sarah sat down and pondered. As she queried in her mind about it, she heard the familiar voice of the Spirit easing her confusion. "My dear Sarah, yes, thought travel is still possible, for those whose bodies have experienced the changes that resurrection have brought to their bodies. In recognition of the many new believers, it is not employed with regularity, but on occasion, because of our love for humanity and our understanding of the intensity of true worship, grace flows and zip, you're there. Rest, my tender one, for every day brings new blessings and new ways to bless others."

Sarah sank into the lounger for a moment and rested her eyes. In the briefest of moments, she was transported to a quiet place, of grandeur untold. At once, she felt absolutely rested and fully exhilarated. She did not even know how to think about this place, or what it was; she only knew it was a place chosen for her. As soon as she acknowledged the thought, it became even more solid in its truth. This place was created for Sarah alone.

Chapter 11
Refuge of Wonder

Sarah was breathless with the beauty around her. It enveloped her and yet she had space to move, to explore. It was replete with color and awash with love. She twirled and danced, as sweet, tender music floated around her. As she bounded with cartwheels and flips, like a school girl gymnast, Sarah giggled in amazement. This was the most fulfilling, blessed place she had ever been. She felt the love soak into her, filling up every tiny cell in her body.

In the midst of exploring this place of wonder, Sarah asked the Lord, "Please, Lord, tell me of this place. I feel so blessed here and have never been here before, yet it is somehow familiar. I don't understand it, but that's how it seems to be. Is there a name for this place? And Lord, what is its purpose?"

In response, with tender love in His eyes, Daddy God came to her and held her hands, then enfolded her in His arms. For a long while, they rested together in love. Then Sarah's Daddy motioned to a fern, who merely bent his leafy appendages to accommodate both of them sitting down, and began to share with her. "You are my precious little one. I created this place for you when you were a tiny child. You first visited here when you perceived it only as a black cloud of safety, during the moments your physical body was being molested. You were so tiny, you didn't even understand what was happening to your body, but merely that it hurt. I prepared this place and helped you to come here, so that the part of you that was really you, your spirit, would remain with me. It was for your safety emotionally, but also for strength to endure physically."

Sarah's eyes grew wide with the remembrance. She remembered the feeling of separating her emotions from the rest of her; she could do nothing about what was being done to her, but she could place herself in this black cloud and be safe. Daddy God continued, with great tenderness in His voice, "Yes, my little one, I helped you to come here and kept your spirit and emotions safe in my love. It was a black cloud because you were not yet thinking in terms of color. The sexual assaults on your body occurred in your first year of life on Earth, before you could talk or walk. You were not able to say, "No!" or walk, or even run away. As the assaults continued, with different assailants throughout your youth, this place of safety remained the same blackness of safety that you were familiar with. We want you to now experience it as it is, with the fullness of color, love, safety, and joy. It is yours; it is for no one else. You are welcome to come as you please, whenever you want to rest alone, yet always in Our Presence and Our Love."

"Oh," Sarah sighed. "Thank you, for helping me when I was so tiny, and for bringing me here now. I am wondering, where is this in the universe? And how big is it? I can see beauty all over, with such colors as I have never seen!"

Daddy God chuckled and responded, "It is actually outside of the universe. It would seem scientifically that there is no end to the universe. But We are outside of the universe because we created it. These unique places We have created for our little ones, who endured such overwhelming trauma within the confines of the universe, are these are places of safety and peace and all are beyond the universe in a dissimilar realm. There is no address here and no one else can come here. It is for you only, for your joy and remembrance of how much you are loved. It is as big as you would like it to be. For here, you are with Us in a very unique way. Here, you are able to create with Us, merely by thinking."

"Oh my, Lord God!" Sarah exclaimed. "I am over-whelmed and in awe of your love." With that, she jumped up and twirled herself in a dizzying frenzy, but felt nothing but pure, sweet joy. She stopped long enough to run up a tree trunk and kick off into a back flip, laughing as she flew over her Daddy God's head, softly landing on her feet amidst a bunch of hydrangea florets. "Oh, I've always wanted to do that!" she giggled. "I feel so loved, so much so that all the pain that once was, is erased by this beauty all around me." Straightaway, she flitted this way and that, stopping momentarily to examine a line of what looked, to Sarah, to be butterflies. She was fascinated because they were linked together by tiny interlocking appendages that looked like arms; they flew in the most beautiful line dance Sarah had ever seen. Their colorful wings made delicate whishing sounds, in tones that were higher for the little ones and deeper for the larger ones. Each was unique, but together, they were a symphony of melodious dance and splashes of color. When they noticed Sarah watching them, they emitted a giggling sound, and their wings fluttered even faster! Sarah smiled wide and twirled before them; they giggled louder and flew in a new line dance pattern to show their joy of interacting with her. She said, "Oh, my little friends, Thank you," and bowed her head just a bit. To her amazement, they slowed their flight, even closing their wings, then resumed their lovely line dancing with renewed vigor.

Sarah took a final twirl, singing to her new friends, "Goodbye, my sweeties!" She finished her swirl, moving right into leaping - to the right and to the left. As she did so, she called out to her Daddy God, "I remember being here and the raw sense of pain that I somehow couldn't shake. Oh, how I love being here now, with this spectacular feeling of movement without pain, with the fanciful freedom that you created my body to give me. Thank you, Daddy God, for this place and for how you have blessed me so!"

Sarah knew she would hear His voice, for He is everywhere at the same time, with her as she explored this new, personal place of blessing. "You are my precious; I am honored that you are enjoying this place. It blesses me just to be with you, Little One." When he called her Little One, her heart leapt with the absolute truth that was infused in the name. It encompassed all of who she was, the little one who experienced suffering in her youth on Earth, the grieving little one who deeply needed the full consolation that only God could give, and the maturing little one who placed her every need, every care, upon the tender care of her Savior, Jesus the Christ. She knew in that moment, that she would ever be God's Little One. It was confirmed by the familiar washing over of the Spirit's love, which tingled all over her body in flushing, powerful love.

Sarah felt entranced by this place of blessing. She remembered thinking about her "black cloud of safety" when she was young, but this place was so much more than that. She lifted her arms and eyes, turning around and around in utter bliss, thinking, I need to re-name this place. I think I'll call it, "Refuge of Wonder." As soon as she said the name in her mind, she knew it was just the right name; it seemed to click into place, like the body shift that she experienced way back during her counseling years. That feeling had felt so confusing when she first experienced it, but it was replete with truth. She had learned to trust it when her own body confirmed to her the absolute truth of her life, what happened to her when she was just a slip of a child, and later, when she began to make positive changes that brought blessing not only to her own life, but to others as well. It's like the phrase she had heard, "You know, that you know, that you know!" That's how it felt when she named this place of grace, "Refuge of Wonder."

The other thing that happened when she named her place surprised her intensely. It was as though God had placed a special notation in her cognizance, of where her Refuge of

Wonder was located. Sarah mused, *"How much this is like the out-of-the-physical-world address of the worldwide web! It is physically here, but for only me! No one else can find it; God has given only me it's very special location!"* She felt like God had even given it special notation, like adding a "★" to a message that's important to remember. She intuitively knew that she would not ever lose the link to where this place was; it was hers forever. *"Wow, forever!"* Sarah thought; she felt utterly satiated.

As if hearing her thoughts, a gorgeous rhododendron bush stretched its delicate pink and fuchsia flowers toward her, several down by her feet, more by her hands and even more in a stair-like position. As Sarah responded to the invitation by putting one foot onto what seemed so beautiful and delicate, the flowers lifted her up, higher and higher. She was delighted and thankful she had one to hold onto! The flowers were so strong, yet they were never marred by her weight. She giggled with abandon, her sweet laughter filled the air. Daddy God giggled too; His delight was His precious daughter reveling in the gift He had given. Sarah began to jump, from one beautiful flower to another, and with each one, the rhododendron bush began to respond in a harmonious tune, sounding something like an oboe, with a reedy thick tone, each flower a different pitch. Soon, Sarah and the bush were dancing to a lively tune. When at last she decided to slow down, the rhododendron eased her to the ground.

Sarah ran back to her Daddy God, threw her arms around His neck and hugged Him as much as she could, singing quietly in His ear,

> "Thank you, Lord, for saving my soul.
> Thank you, Lord, for making me whole.
> Thank you, Lord, for giving to me,
> Your great salvation, so rich and free."

Daddy God sang back to her, holding her gently to Him, "I will love you with an everlasting love, my Little One."

Sarah just rested in His lap, soaking in His love. Though she felt so totally filled with His love, she never tired of receiving it. As a little girl, she had thought it was all she ever needed. This place that once was her only place of safety. In reality, it has always been a holy place, for her Daddy God and His Little One to share. So precious a gift it was, that she would always cherish it. After a bit, Daddy God expounded, "This is a place for your fancy; whatever you desire, it will come to pass. I know your heart and it is pure before me. I know that you will not squander this place, as someone who would trash it like a foolish child. Colors and scents are free for you to imagine and compose. The creativity will be complimented by my blessing upon it and everything you imagine, will be. We will unite as we join together in the fellowship of this place. It is for you and us; it may be Jesus that you want to share something with and He will accompany you. Or perhaps, you may come here alone and the Spirit may join you, as we rejoice together of life, love, and grace."

Sarah breathed again, as she rested her head on his chest, "Oh, thank you, Daddy God. I honor you and praise you, for I have been fearfully and wonderfully made, just as the beauty here in this place. I will cherish it." She closed her eyes and rested in His love.

Beyond time and space, Sarah was transported back to Earth, to her sweet abode. She smiled, as she touched down just in front of the gorgeous ribbon bouquet. It had even deeper meaning now, reminding her of her Refuge of Wonder and the joy she could experience there any time she wanted. She puttered around, eating and drinking leisurely and relaxing in the glow of such high and holy blessings she had received.

Thus, the days flowed, marked only by the rising and setting of the sun and moon, and the wonderful surging of

Jesus' blessings in the midst of activities. Sarah felt that she was acclimatizing to the newness of life with Jesus, back on Earth; He brought healing to not only humanity, but also the air, water, and land. Every animal and plant flourished with His blessing; the beauty reverberated Sarah's senses, especially the colors and fragrances. Every day was new; every experience refreshingly pleasurable.

The new believers grew in their faith and were blessed with many children, who grew and learned of Jesus firsthand. They still had their own freedom to choose to follow Jesus. Those who chose to follow Him, grew in faith and expression of Jesus' love in their hearts and minds. Those who did not, grew in the negatives of their own hearts. Even though Satan himself and his demons were bound and in the abyss, the dredges of Satan's influence still drug down their spirits, into depression, self-pity, anger, and even violence.

These children became restless in the community of faith and banded together in gangs. They were so uncomfortable that they chose to leave Jerusalem and became wild, range-roving boys and girls. They foraged for their food and fed every desire they conceived in their minds.

One day, after some years had passed, Sarah felt the strong pull to go with Sally outside the community of believers, to share Jesus' love with the children. With the assurance of the Spirit, that Jesus would accompany her and Sally, and a quick affirmation from her dear friend, Sarah prepared a fruit smoothie to refresh herself for the journey.

Chapter 12
To the Hurting, Broken Children

Sarah, Sally, and Jesus walking briskly, toward the northwest and the Mediterranean Sea. Jesus knew the children were camped along the shore. He shared with Sarah and Sally, "There are many of these who are weary of their lifestyle, which is devoid of joy." He breathed in deeply, praying silently to His Father in Heaven for the little ones, rebellious though they may be. Then He continued, "We have these letters from their parents," slapping the rucksack on his back, "to soften their hearts about the families they have left. I know the deep need of every single one of them and I have great compassion for them, not condemnation."

Sarah was thankful for her renewed body, for she and Sally had to jog to keep up with the pace Jesus set; they could feel the urgency and love Jesus exuded. He whispered, seemingly letting go of the fact of their presence with Him, "Oh my Father, prepare their hearts to receive me. You know my longing for their precious souls. Each one we have loved from before creation; bring to their hearts a longing for our love." All at once, at the end of His prayer, Jesus dropped to His knees, almost sending Sarah and Sally toppling end over end, so close were they to Him. They too, kneeled and prayed silently. A gentleness settled over them, a sweet peace that felt like melted caramel. At length they rose, then Jesus too. He thanked them, "I appreciate so much your sensitivity; my heart has been heavy for these little ones and now it is light, for the Spirit is preparing their hearts for the love of God to reign in their souls. It is a day of great joy. Come, let us gather the harvest for life eternal!"

Once again, Jesus led them briskly. However, this time, there was a spring in His step, like he had actual springs at the bottom of His sandals. Sarah found her steps more buoyant with the joy that was ahead. Sally, too, felt the physical blessing of joy and bounded ahead with gusto. Sally was so happy to be on this very special journey with Jesus that she broke into song,

> "Jesus loves the little children,
> all the children of the world
> Red and yellow, black and white;
> they are precious in His sight.
> Jesus loves the little children of the world."

Soon they were all singing, in a round, which Sarah had always loved, each singing the same song, but starting at different times. It felt like a party, just knowing the children's hearts were being prepared for the love of all the universe to reign in their hearts. They bounded down the well-worn trail, singing and laughing! Sarah thought, *"A finer day, I've never had!"*

The children had heard them singing; when they crested a rise, then turned down a sloping curve, they came upon the huge group of children. They were dirty, with tattered clothes and hearts yearning for love. Sarah and Sally saw the despair in their faces and her heart was broken for them. Jesus not only saw their despair, but felt it as well. He said, "Come, I have letters from your parents. He sat down on a boulder with a flat spot, took off the ruck sack and opened it up. He pulled the letters out, one at a time and said the name upon each letter, "Jess", "Elmo", "Samantha". Jesus spoke their names with such compassion and love that each wall that had been built against Him crumbled. With each name that Jesus said, little hands grasped for the hope of tender love from a parent, very timid at first. But then, a boldness took ahold of the group, as each child received their letter and opened them. Some began to cry with the love that poured off the pages and into their hearts. The last of the children stood around Jesus with their hands open and eyes burning with tears, even before receiving their letters.

One little girl came to Sarah and asked if she would read her letter to her. "I never learned to read," she said, her head hanging in sadness.

Sarah said, "Oh yes, of course, I will." With sweet tenderness, she read to the little girl the words her mother had written,

"My sweet little Amber, I want you to know how precious you are to your father and me. We were overjoyed to have you be a part of our family. You brought so much joy to our home, with your giggles and tickles. We have missed you and pray that you will return to us and we will be a family once again. We understand that you were drawn away and may have not even understood what was happening to you. We are not upset with you, but we love you with all our hearts. You are our sweetness! Your father and I pray for you every day that you will come back to us. Love you so… Mom"

When Sarah finished reading the letter, she looked into the eyes of a child so bereft of joy that her face looked morose. Sarah ached to give this child a hug, to bring hope and love into her life. She asked the sweet little thing, "Amber, may I hug you?"

Amber nodded her tiny head, with tears finally escaping her eyes. Sarah enfolded the slight child in her arms, lifting her to hold her on her lap. Amber cried softly, holding tightly the letter from her mother, as she was cradled and loved. She stayed a long time, finding the peace she needed in the arms of a compassionate lady.

Jesus gazed at these dear broken children. He knew their private pains and the struggle they've had just to survive. The oldest boys and girls were in their late teens and the youngest was just five years old, only a whisp of a girl. He lifted his hands and motioned for everyone to come near, while saying, "Come and join me for a story; I have a doosy to tell you!" The children sat in a broad semi-circle on a blanket of grass and wildflowers. Jesus began, "When I was a young man, I healed men and women, boys and girls, from the sicknesses in their bodies. Wherever I went, people followed me, lots of people. One day, I was sharing about the Kingdom of God. The particular story I was sharing was about sheep. A man had lots of sheep, but one day, one of the lambs got lost. He left the entire heard of sheep to go find the little lost lamb. He found the little fella caught up in a bramble of prickly vines. The man helped the little lamb get away from the thorns and carried him all the way back to the heard. The best part of that story is how it is like the Kingdom of God. When God finds the one who is lost, and brings him home, oh, there is great rejoicing in heaven. I am the Lord, I am Jesus and I have come to bring you home. Will you receive me? Will you come home with me and be my precious children? I love each one of you; you are cherished. I have loved you from before you were even born."

One little guy jumped to his feet and lifted his fist in victory, exclaiming, "Yes, I want you and I need you. Please forgive me of all the rotten stuff I've done." He ran to Jesus, jumping over his friends' heads, as they sat on the ground, and into Jesus arms. Jesus blessed him, "Ben, I do forgive you; in fact, you will be a strong leader to whom many people will learn from." Ben jumped on the back of the rock and onto Jesus' back, putting both of his scruffy arms around Jesus neck. Jesus jumped up, to Ben's delight, and said, "Who's that on my back?" With everyone guffawing loudly, Jesus finally found who had him, He just ducked and leaned over with his right shoulder down, reaching with His right hand and swinging him around to hug him tight.

Ben giggled and hugged Him back. He said, "Jesus, I love you." Then he jumped to the ground and said to all his buddies, "Hey guys, it's OK! Jesus loves us and that's OK with me!" He threw his left arm out in a wide arc and reiterated the invitation, "Come on, guys!" One at a time, the kids stood up and made their way to Jesus. He welcomed them, forgave each one, loved them and blessed greatly every single child.

"They were lost," Sarah mused, *"but now they're found."* She and Sally hugged the children as they finished with Jesus. Even little Amber responded and ran to Jesus, receiving Him as her Lord. *"It was the most beautiful of afternoons,"* Sarah pondered.

When at last Jesus finished blessing every child, He motioned for them all to sit down again. Then He shared with them the miracle of His provision. First, Jesus told the story from His early ministry, "When so many people followed me out of the town, and I blessed them and healed so many of their illnesses, it took a long while. People were starting to get hungry. Are you hungry now, just like they were? There was a little boy who was willing to share his lunch. Well, there were 5,000 men and most of them had brought their families that day, so there were a lot of hungry people and only 2 fish and 5 loaves of bread. I took the basket of fish and bread and gave thanks to God the Father, who is in Heaven, and blessed the bread and fish for the nourishment of the people. Then the fish and bread were put into baskets and passed out; everyone took all that they needed and there were 12 baskets of food left over!"

The kids hollered, "Wow!" and "Way Cool!" and "I'm sure hungry too!"

Jesus then got to the fun part. He asked for Sally to bring the sandwich and apple that she had brought for lunch. He shared with the kids, "OK, kids. Do you want to not only see a miracle, but be a part of one?" Amid the shouts of affirmation, Jesus said, "OK, here it goes. First we give thanks. So, everyone bow before the God of Heaven and Earth. 'Father God, we thank you for this gift for our lunch, a granny smith sour apple and a peanut butter and raspberry jam sandwich. We ask you Father, to bless this food and multiply it, for the blessing of all our bodies. We thank you for blessing these children today. May it be a day they will remember with fun and delight. Amen.' "

All the children together said "Amen!" and sat in rapt attention to watch the miracle unfold for lunch. Jesus cut the sandwich in half and then the apple in quarters, coring each section, then placed one section of the apple in each of four baskets. The children drew in their breath when Jesus place a half PB & J in each of the four baskets. Then the baskets were passed from both sides of the group, near the front and both sides from the back. During the short walk from Jesus to the first children to take their lunch from the baskets, the meager sandwich and apple slices multiplied and the baskets were filled with PB & J's and apple quarters. The children "Ooooh'd" and "Ahhhhh'd" and exclaimed, "Wow!" as they munched their favorite lunch until they were completely satiated.

Sarah and Sally had picked up the four baskets and there were still a lot of sandwich halves and apple quarters for them and Jesus. At length, Jesus stood and patted his belly, saying, "That was good! I feel like a walk; anyone want to hike with me and the ladies here (indicating Sarah and Sally with a sweep of His hand) back to Jerusalem?"

All the kids joined in a unanimous "Yes!" Jacob, one of the older boys said, "Lord Jesus, we'll need only a few minutes to gather up our stuff." Turning toward the kids, he exclaimed, "Hey, guys, we're going home! Let's see how quick we can clean up camp and pack up!" The children scattered in a frenetic pace to return with Jesus to Jerusalem and to their parents. Rather than merely waiting, Sarah and Sally helped the littlest ones to gather their belongings, placing them in home-made bags the children had fashioned from woven jasmine vines and large Jerusalem artichoke leaves. Sarah marveled how the children had cared for each other so well; they were like a big family.

Little Amber told Sarah she had a secret to tell her. Sarah gingerly bent low and Amber whispered in her ear, "I'm so glad you, Sally, and Jesus came when you did. The older kids were mean, to each other, and to us younger ones. I can feel Jesus' love in my heart and now I see how all the kids are different – all at once!"

Sarah responded in hushed whispers as well, "Yes, Jesus' love changes us from the inside out! He forgives all the bad things we've done in the past and helps us to live in His love. We no longer want to hurt each other. I am so thankful all of you received Him. Would you like me to carry you on my shoulders on the walk back to Jerusalem, Amber?"

Amber smiled a big, toothless grin and nodded. She finished putting all her nature toys, which she had made herself, into the bag, then all her hand-me-down clothes that she had from the other kids in the group. Finally, she rolled her tattered blanket and lumpy pillow, tying it together with a vine-rope. She announced in her tiny, squeaky voice, "I'm ready!"

Sarah sat down on the stump that she had sat on during lunch and suggested, "How about if we just sit here a minute and watch what is happening with all the other kids?"

Amber joined her on the stump; it was a huge stump, of an age-old olive tree. She leaned her head against Sarah's arm and let go of a huge sigh, as the weight of her burdened heart had been lifted and she could relax and enjoy being a child again.

In amazing rapidity, all the children gathered together, with various bags jammed by their meager possessions, ready for the trek back to their families. Sarah lifted Amber onto her shoulders and Sally lifted another little one on hers. The kids giggled as they settled in for the ride. The older kids ran races with Jesus, jumped into His arms and hooted with the hilarity of their new-found love and peace. Their hearts were bursting with joy and their antics displayed it. The hike back to Jerusalem was swallowed up in the absolute joy of the love of God as expressed in these young lives.

As they entered the outskirts of Jerusalem, there was great rejoicing, for the Spirit had encouraged the families to come and meet their children. The whole community was there to rejoice with them. A few of the families had prepared food and Jesus blessed the food and in another miracle, multiplied it for all to receive a physical manifestation of His love.. Families reunited with hugs and kisses and playful games. The joy of family, in the love of God, ruled the day. Sally and Sarah felt so much a part of that blessing that they fell right into the revelry, playing, running, chasing, hugging, and loving every minute.

After hours of fun and rejoicing, families began to gather their things and head for home. The children came to Sarah and Sally and thanked them, hugging them. Amber whispered to Sarah, "You are always going to be my bestest friend!"

"Ah, and you will always be my best friend," hugging her little friend tenderly. Mothers and fathers also had tender hugs for Sally and Sarah, for their gifts of kindness to their children.

Jesus also blessed the children again, taking time for each child and each family. He loved on them like no other, filling their deepest need with profound love. Once more, He blessed Sally and Sarah, scooping them up by the waist, one in each arm, and twirling them around as everyone laughed. Sarah adored the fun of being with her Lord; every moment was blessed with His love. Most often, she was quite overwhelmed by the power of His love flowing over her. It fulfilled her in ways she had not even known were possible.

When Jesus released the gals, they were breathless with laughing so hard and had to relax a moment just to gather their bearings. With a wave of love and grace, Jesus strolled toward town. Sally suggested they sit down and just rest a moment; Sarah merely nodded and they sank into a sweet pile of moss.

Chapter 13
New Every Morning

The days and nights flew by, with a whirlwind of activity and blessing. Sarah observed one day, even though it had been slowly happening over the years, an atypical maturing in humanity. No one's body grew to be old, with pain, lessening of physical and mental abilities, nor were there any illnesses. Those whose bodies had been perfected on Resurrection Morning remained in youthful adulthood; those who had lived in Heaven either retained their choice of living as a youngster, or maturing to be a young adult. Those who had been born since matured naturally to adulthood, but then the aging eased off altogether. The scourge of illness death were gone.

Sarah pensively followed through with her thoughts, *"Most of us appreciate the wonderful way we feel and rejoice in Christ, who has made provision for life abundant. But there are a few who refuse to accept Jesus' love and provision; yet they too experienced total health, until such time that the Lord holds all of humanity – from throughout all of history – accountable for their choices and actions. Oh, how I love His grace, for He has forgiven and forgotten all my sins!"*

Sarah and Sally assisted Jesus with new believers, relishing the blessings that flowed over the body of Christ with the flickering of faith. The power and love of Jesus fanned it into deep, maturing, profound faith. In the process, the two gals matured to a level unfathomable and more intuitive than either would have imagined possible. When thinking about it, Sarah mused, *"With God, everything is possible!"* and breathed a "Thank You, Father!" for all the blessings that had been given her. Every day seemed better than the last; family and friends frolicked in the absolute beauty of Jerusalem. Sarah had time, an abundance of time, to cherish moments with every loved one. In fact, she came to love everyone with a powerful love. It was the utopia she had dreamed of when climbing a tall evergreen in her youth, so long ago.

Day and night, moment by moment, refreshing life poured into Sarah, filling her with a renewed awe of just how wonderfully God had made humanity. The early part of her life reflected only a miniscule amount of all that God had built into humanity. It had been diminished by sin, torn into bits by self-focus and pride. Jesus' love was poured over humanity, as He paid the penalty for that sin and restored not only humanity, but also relationship with the Creator, Sustainer, and Comforter.

Sarah pondered the absolute fullness of humanity; her body was strong, lithe, comfortable, devoid of pain, and well, beautiful too. Everyone and everything exuded the beauty of God's love. *"Most fascinating,"* Sarah thought, *"is the ability of my body to take in more and more of God's love and blessings and not explode with the sheer pressure of it all!"*

Sarah rested a bit more, just breathing deep of the Lord Jesus. Even now, her every breath was a gift of the grace of God. She had so much gratitude for the gift of life itself that she could hardly contain it. She wanted to give a gift to her Lord that would be worthy of all that He has done for her. She felt that nothing could describe her thankfulness sufficiently. She remembered bringing gifts to her daddy when she was a very little tyke, made with her love all mixed in with paint, glue, and glitter. Even though they were not well made, the fact that her love was intricately involved in the making gave them immense value to her papa.

"Exactly the same here," whispered the Spirit of God, "the simplest of gifts has inestimable value because your love is in every aspect."

"Oh, thank you, my Lord," sighed Sarah. "I know I cannot make or do anything that is enough, but with my love included, you are blessed. I want to bless you and honor you every moment, every day."

As a confirmation of the love of God for Sarah, the Spirit introduced a new thought to her, through a picture of pretty white flowers. Sarah saw in her mind the morning glory vine, with its beautiful cone shaped flowers. She heard the Spirit's gentle wisdom, "Every morning, there is a new flower blooming. That particular flower only lasts for only one day; the next morning another flower will open with renewed beauty. For humanity and angelity, the Father, Son, and I are always the same, like the vine itself. But we are also new every morning, even every moment, similar to seeing a new floral beauty with the new day. Our love is a constant, but the expression of it is endlessly new. Our love for you cannot grow, for it is already at the greatest fullness, well beyond your human capacity for comprehension. For this reason, every day, there will be new expressions of our love for you to experience. From your perspective, our love is new every morning. From ours, that love is eternal and more profound then even can be held in all of creation."

Sarah pondered the wonder of God's love. She lifted her arms and hands high in worship; with her eyes closed and embraced the truth that was revealed to her by the Spirit. She said the phrase, "You love and compassion are new every morning," over and over, remembering her Bible study back home. She remembered it well, from Lamentations, but could not grasp its meaning fully until the moment the Spirit revealed it to her. She felt like a window opened up in her mind, one that was obscured before. Sarah felt like she was rushing down a river of love, with the white water of excitement filling her inner spirit. She realized that life with the Lord would never be boring, nor would she ever feel sad, depressed, nor all the other negatives of her past. Life with the Triune God would always be exhilarating, loving, and absolutely bursting of fulfilled hope. She remembered praying for years, seeking the Lord's face with her entire being, on behalf of one she loved. Every prayer she ever prayed had been answered by the One who holds all of creation in its place. She had been able to experience for herself, the blessings that had come about in the lives of family and friends - from the foundation of prayer that she had been committed to.

As Sarah worshipped, she let go of herself and experienced almost the same feeling she had back on Resurrection Morning as she let go of her old body, clothes and all, and was given her new, eternally healthy body. The Lord lifted her spirit above everything, to an emotional place of fellowship with the Triune God. Sarah felt giddy with the intense unity with Daddy God, Savior and Brother, Jesus, and the Spirit of the Eternal God. It was not a physical place, but rather, purely emotional and deeply fulfilling. Oh, how she felt loved! She realized that the love she felt was reflected in color, which swirled and played a game of beauty and love all around her. There were vibrant colors which she had never seen, but they held a boldness of love that radiated and pierced into her emotional self. Sarah did not have the words to describe how she felt, but she knew immediately that God knew, and was pleased that she had been blessed so overwhelmingly.

As she returned to her body, she felt the Holy Spirit whispering again in His gentle way. He murmured, "My sweet Sarah, as you mature in our love, we will share more of these precious fellowship times with you. It is the ultimate in relationship, to have this emotional connection with you. Be blessed my dear."

Sarah spoke softly, with joy filling her spirit, "Oh, thank you, my Lord and my God." Again, she rested for a moment, allowing the intensity of the emotional fellowship to subside just a bit. She mused, *"Yes, the Lord's love is new every morning. Wow, this has been so powerful, so profound!"* Then she had another thought bounce around in her head, *"Moreover, His love and the expression of it is new every moment! So many things happen every day, with every activity and every individual; the love of God infuses life itself with moment by moment blessing!"*

As she pondered these truths, Sarah felt like a soft, warm blanket enveloped her in a grace-filled affirmation of the truths she had received. She thought back to the weird feelings of Earth that she remembered having, a type of disjointed feeling of being in the physical world that was fallen and profuse with pain and at the very same time, leaning so much on the Lord for her emotional and spiritual strength. Now, every aspect of life oozed the love and grace of the Lord Jesus; there was nothing disjointed about life with her Lord!

"New every morning," the tender Spirit had said. Sarah experienced it and more, ever blessed in relationships with her family, friends, and the ever expanding body of believers. Years flowed, like a river of blessing, never ending. Sarah never aged and never tired of the daily fun and excitement of living with her Lord.

Early one morning, Sarah leaned back upon the lounging chair, closing her eyes and resting. She pondered all the wonders she had seen and experienced since Resurrection Morning. Every moment replayed in her mind, with such vivid detail that she felt the feelings with the same, or even more, intensity as when they first occurred. However, the memories were almost instantaneous in nature. Sarah thought, *"It's almost like watching a video in fast forward, but better because I know every detail and feel all the emotions!"*

Thinking of all these blessings brought Sarah's family to her mind. She wondered how they were faring and reflected, "It's about time for a great family reunion; I think I'll take a walk and see what happens!"

Chapter 14
High and Holy Blessings

Rejuvenated and excited for the new day of blessings, Sarah bounded out of her Earth abode and stretched out her arms and legs, breathing deep of the sweet Mediterranean air. She realized with a start, "Oh my, how wonderful it is that Jesus has been healing the Earth of its pollutants and scars that humanity wrought upon it!" Even after the many hundred years of living back on Earth, every day, it was cleaner, fresher, and produced all manner of healthy food for them to eat.

The Spirit of God whispered to her heart and mind, "Go up on Mount Olivet, for I have a high blessing for your family there."

With exhilarating expectation, Sarah stepped into a quick paced hike to the holy mountain. With alternating steps, she breathed in, "Yah" and out, "weh." Every time she entered into this simple exercise, she was blessed with the full knowledge that her very breath, as well as all her bodily functions, was by the matchless grace and love of God. On this morning, she added, "Your love is" and "new every morning." She felt energized and strong. Along the way, she passed the marketplace, the temple, and the abundant gorgeous foliage that flourished in the renewed health of the planet. She paused, almost planting her face in the floral abundance and breathing deep of their luscious aromas.

Sarah arrived at the foothills of Mount Olivet and caught sight of several of her kids, Mark and John, roughhousing for fun, as they transversed the hillside. She looked further up the mountain side and watched her parents, Nancy and William, as they ascended the holy mountain. She observed in awe, as she pensively considered their new lives of health, peace, and joy; what an absolute turn-around from the constant anger and dysfunction of their relationship before the love of Christ entered in!

Sarah realized that the Lord had called all of her family for this blessing. Not only did she see her kids and her parents, but her siblings as well; Leroy and Timothy were racing to the top in a brotherly challenge. Her sister, Elizabeth, and her three younger brothers, Lester, Ty were climbing together, holding hands with their arms stretched out, the guys pulling Elizabeth from either side and then giggling, as she tried to pull both of them on up the hillside.

Sarah looked to the other direction, to her right and there were a bunch more! Randy, her youngest brother, was almost to the top; he looked small because he was so far from where she stood, at the foothills. Her daughter, Linda, frolicked in the mass of burgeoning flowering shrubs about halfway down the slope, running around one, then another, and back around the first! Sarah giggled at the sight of her sweet daughter enjoying herself so much. Charlotte and Pearl were making slow progress in a game of skipping up the hillside. Sarah thought, *"My sweet grandchild is chock-full of fun and delight!"*

Pure elation bounded up the hill with Sarah, drawing her in an inexplicable excitement; she knew blessings awaited them all at the top of this honorable mountain. She considered thought-travel to the top, but decided the climb would be fun. She angled toward Paul, who was also just beginning the climb. Seeing his warm smile made her heart flutter with their continuing deep, profound friendship.

Sarah responded, "Hello, my favorite guy! How are you doing, this beautiful morning?"

Paul, replied, "I'm doing great! I sure love living back on Earth with Jesus! He makes everything better every single day!"

Sarah agreed with a colossal smile and a tender hug. Paul suggested, "Let's link arms and climb, stepping together!" Paul put out his arm and Sarah slid her arm under and around her fella's. "OK," Paul guided, "Now, we'll start with the right leg." Within a couple of steps, they were climbing arm-in-arm, legs-in-sync. Then Paul added something else to the mix. He said, "Now, to make this even more fun, and more complicated, let's sing! We have to keep in step, but what would be a good song?" Sarah thought a moment, then said, "I know! Let's sing 'Fairest Lord Jesus' " and began in her warm alto voice; Paul joined in with his light baritone vocals. Together the harmony was captivatingly beautiful:

> "Fairest Lord Jesus, Ruler of all nature,
> O Thou of God and man the Son,
> Thee will I cherish, Thee will I honor,
> Thou, my soul's glory, joy and crown."

As they began next stanza, other familiar voices joined in the beautiful hymn, lifting their voices high in the hillside as they climbed its slopes,

> "Fair are the meadows, fairer still the woodlands,
> Robed in the blooming garb of spring;
> Jesus is fairer, Jesus is purer,
> Who makes the woeful heart to sing."

Sarah mused, as the last phrase gave her pause, "*Oh, wow! There is no longer any woeful heart; there is only joy and singing is a huge expression of that joy!*"

The lovely hymn diminished in the wind, until the blended voices were completely carried away from the mountain the family had scaled. Sarah had been so enthralled by the song that she had not even glanced around as they rounded the sloping crest of the Mount of Olives. As she slowly turned around now, she beheld the grandeur of not only the holy mountain, but as far as she could see, the surrounding countryside. She perused all of

Jerusalem and the adjacent suburbs and reflected on the history and current changes of this place. For centuries, Mount Olivet itself had become an expansive cemetery. When Jesus came back to the Earth and vegetation once again flourished, olive groves were once again cultivated amid floral abundance; this honorable mountain exudes the holiness with which God imbued it.

For generations, Jerusalem had been a city of conflict, tension, and violence; now, the centuries of conflict were over. Peace reigned, with Jesus at its helm. With millions of Christ-followers in its midst, Jerusalem and the surrounding lands had become huge suburbs of reverberating elation. Wherever she looked, Sarah saw sprawling communities – no pollution hovering in the sky or revolting aromas rising from the ground.

Sarah observed a remarkable aspect of the view before her; there was a holy effervescence that hovered over the Earth. She hadn't noticed it when she was in the valley area, but just above the valley floor, she could see the covering, which blanketed the Earth with love. She was just beginning to formulate the beginnings of a question, when she received the answer from the Spirit.

He shared in a serene whisper, "Yes, this is my Holy Presence hovering over the land. Just as Jesus shares healing love with humanity and with the Earth, my Presence hovers and covers over all people. Where there once was discord, there is now absolute peace and great joy."

Sarah and Paul treasured the moment together, both worshipping the Holy One. Paul said, "It sure is wonderful! Wow! The love of God hovering over us! I love being here and I love being with you, Sarah."

"Me too," Sarah replied. "As much as we love each other, God loves us way beyond that! I think He's going to show us just a smidgen of how much!" She squeezed Paul's hand and gave it a swing right over their heads, indicating her excitement. Paul joined in and soon, their arms were going 'round and 'round in a playful expression of their affection for each other.

As Sarah and Paul scanned the beauty spread out before them, William and Nancy came from behind and hugged them both at the same time, a surprise hug! Sarah giggled and Paul released a big, happy sigh. Then, with everyone arriving at the summit of the mountain, they all made their way to a huge garden gazebo, which was adorned with fuchsia, lavender, and light pink wisteria that draped themselves beautifully all over the structure. Surrounding the gazebo was a rock garden, with all manner of precious gemstones placed in curves that swirled all over in a gorgeous walkway. Sarah and Paul walked all around the gazebo, gazing at the beauty and workmanship of the walkway.

After traversing the entire circumference of the gazebo, Sarah ambled up the wide steps of the gazebo and joined the family. Comfortable lounge chairs, with beautiful tapestry cushions, offered beauty and comfort. She sank into the nearest one; with Paul sitting right next to her. He enveloped her in a tender hug and whispered "It was fun coming up here with you!" into her ear. She replied, "It sure was, love you!" She felt so safe in his arms, like a tenderly-cared-for sister in grace. She marveled at the depth of their friendship; thinking back to the pre-rapture life as husband and wife, she had never imagined having an eternal friendship as profound as they now shared.

Straightaway after her hug with Paul, Sarah felt the arms of another man cover her shoulders; she had this hug from behind and had no idea who was hugging her! She had to just receive the love, then when released, she turned around to see who it was. Oh, was she surprised! It was Leroy, her brother. Oh, how he loved to tease her! Ina flash, the fullness of all that God had done filled her thoughts. *"Life is so very good, with Jesus healing all wounds, all strife; He replaces all the negatives of the fallen nature of mankind with profound forgiveness and life-changing fellowship with God and my loved ones.*" When she finally freed Leroy, they both grinned and without even a moment to think about it, jumped into the crazy "Chicken Dance" that they had done on roller skates years before. Everyone erupted in laughter at the sight! The rest of the family added the tune; they "Chicken Danced" until they were both breathless. Applause rang out, with laughter abounding.

Sarah began hugging everyone; she felt so honored to be in the precious family into which she was born and be with the family she and Paul had been blessed to have. Hugs, kisses, and laughter filled the gazebo up; even the flowers responded to the joy of the morning, releasing their sweet aromas to bless the family even more. At length, all hugged out, everyone sank into the comfortable chairs. Sarah had just taken a deep breath of the fragrant mountain air, when Jesus came walking up the steps and into the allure of the blossom-filled mountain retreat. As each of the family members noticed Him, various responses rever-berated in the gazebo. They sighed, hollered out their joy, and some even jumped up to greet Him in exuberant hugs. Sarah heaved a sigh, overwhelmed with a longing for even more of Him and more of His profound grace. His love fulfilled her in a way she couldn't even express. She knew there were blessings coming for her and her family, but the only thing she could really think about was how much she loved being with Jesus. She remembered longing to see Him, back before the Resurrection Morning; now He was here, with her family, blessing them all with His great love.

Jesus invited them to receive a new blessing, "My dear brothers and sisters, I want to bless you today, each of you individually and as a family. You have overcome all the obstacles that Satan threw at you; I am honored by your faith in me. You are a blessing to myself and to others. Today, I will infuse even more of my love into your lives.

Are you prepared to receive? Do you want more joy, more love?"

Everyone, including Sarah, bellowed out, "Yes, yes, we are ready! We want more love, more joy!" Then they laughed and laughed, so hard they began rolling around on the floor, for their blessing had already begun. The laughter was not from a funny joke, nor a funny story; it was a holy laughter that caught them all by surprise, rising up from deep within. Laughter that made them realize that laughing in the holiness of God, in the Presence of His Spirit, was what laughter was created for. It wasn't stiff, or stilted, but uncontrollable, uproarious guffawing that no one wanted to squelch. At long last, the laughter waned, and a gentle peace descended upon them. Where each person was, laying on the floor of the gazebo, sitting on a chair, or leaning over the side of the gazebo, the peace brought a stillness, a longing for the touch of the Spirit's love to never be over, wafting in the thoughts of all the family members.

Jesus' intense baritone voice resonated with honor,

> 'Fountain of holiness, wisdom and light,
> Sea of all goodness and justice and right,
> River of joy and the riches of life,
> Our Father, our God!'

He continued, in prayer, "Father, I feel your blessing pouring over this family, like a warm blanket of love. Your blessing is both individual, for each of your precious chosen ones here this morning, and corporate, for the entire family to receive together. Your love is profound and so intimate! As we are one in love, so we are united in love with each individual here. Father, let's bless them mightily!"

The whole family had entered into prayer with Jesus, closing their eyes to focus their thoughts on the Holy communication within the Godhead. They had no clue as to the blessing that was about to come upon them. They merely breathed deep, as Jesus' prayer to Father God initiated a whirlwind of a blessing! With a rush of birds' wings, an innumerable amount of feathered friends carrying flowers of every variety whooshed into the gazebo, dropping them on laps, heads, arms, and all over the gazebo. The bouquet of enormous proportion grew even more, as birdies continued to fly in, drop their load of flowers upon the deepening pile, and fly on. They twittered in loud proclamation as they did this, for they felt honored to participate in a blessing of the Lord. When at last the final bird swooped in with huge dahlias held tight in his talons and let go of them, there were so many flowers all over that they gently landed, with no sound. The eagle lunged into a rapid circle above those who had been blessed, as if checking to make sure that the job was well done. It was, for the family was quite overwhelmed by the absolute beauty that covered and surrounded them. It felt like all the beauty and love of God brought them into a truly mountaintop experience, one they would always cherish.

Jesus merely stood and reached forth his hands, to bless them in new waves of bliss, until Sarah was so satiated that she felt she may burst! Every single person in the family was so blessed that they merely lay back their heads, throwing their arms down and to the sides, and just received. No thought of time, nor how they looked, nor even trying to describe this experience in their minds, arose in anyone's mind. When at last the waves of love abated, after a few minutes of soaking in the precious love of God, the family began to sit up and gather the flowers and put them in seven huge vases that adorned the indoor edges of the gazebo. The fragrance tantalized their nostrils with sweet headiness.

As they fit the last of the flowers in the gorgeous vessels, the birds flew back and began to sing together, twilling and twitting each in a unique song and yet, in stunning unison.

Jesus asked Nancy if she would like to dance; she responded with a nod and they waltzed around the gazebo. After only a moment, all the family paired up and danced together, brothers and sisters in Christ, with Christ! They switched partners over and over and danced on, expressing in their movements the joy of their hearts. When the birds' warbling finally subsided, the family applauded them. They had alighted on the railing of the gazebo - three and four deep, for their beautiful concert. Altogether they bowed before Jesus and this family of God, their beaks touching the wood railing. It was the sweetest display of honoring the Lord Jesus that Sarah had ever witnessed!

After the dancing, everyone sat once again and started talking about the blessings of the day, interrupting and talking over each other in their exuberance of the mountaintop blessing. Jesus lifted his arms and said, "Here is some food." Sarah looked and there were two magnificent horses, bearing baskets of fruit, sweet raisin cakes, and nectar in tall carafes, all packed safely for the journey up the hill by another family of God, in their gentle blessing of the Lord Jesus and their brothers and sisters.

William, Mark, Paul, John, Leroy, Lester, Ty, and Randy all stepped down from the gazebo to take the foodstuffs off the horses and into the gazebo. Jesus strode over to the two equines and stroked their manes, necks, and shoulders, appreciating them for their willingness to serve. They brayed in unison, a deep guttural, "We ahhhhhhner youuuuuuuuu, oooooooooour Loooooooord." With a lingering hug for each one, Jesus released them to munch on the lush grass of the mountaintop haven.

He returned to the beloved inside, in just the right moment to offer His blessing upon the food. He lifted both arms and proclaimed, "I bless this food to all our bodies, for strengthening, energy, and abundance." Then, Jesus took an apple, sat down, and began munching the crisp fruit. Sarah and all her family dove into the great provision, each finding just the right thing to satisfy their appetite.

Sarah's dear sister, Elizabeth, whom she had clung to as a youngster and appreciated as a mentor in things of faith as a young adult, stepped up and began munching on one of the sweet raisin cakes. She commented, especially to the other ladies in the family, "I so love our resurrection bodies; we can enjoy this absolutely wonderful food and know that it won't collect any longer on our hips!"

The response was jovial; "Amens" rang out all over the gazebo, along with some "Ah's" and "Mm's." Sarah laughed and said, "Amen to that!" with far more than a smidge of thankfulness.

Her mother observed, "We all look more beautiful and healthy than before Resurrection Morning! And we can enjoy this wonderful food!"

Linda pipped up, "I just love the sweets! Thank you, Jesus, for such morsels for our enjoyment!" Bounteous laughter filled the air. John scooped up his sister, with an arm about her waist, and twirled her around in his merriment. Pearl, who had grown to be a beautiful young lady, said, "Me too, me too!" John set Linda down and only a moment later, was twirling Pearl too. John had a great time twirling each one around and around and loved the squeals. Soon, everyone was swinging around, munching more, and having great fun. Sarah thought, *It's nice that the gazebo is so large. There's still room for everyone to get to the tables with the luscious food.*

Jesus was finally able to get in a reply to Linda's appreciation for the sweet cakes. His grin never faded, as He said vociferously, "It is a joy to bless everyone; this is what life is, experiencing the very best, all the time, in great fellowship together."

Sarah was reminded of a childhood song, from Charlie Brown fame, and began quietly to sing the sweet melody,

"Happiness is morning and evening,
daytime and nighttime too.
for happiness is anyone and anything at all
that's loved by you."

As she sang, in her rich alto voice, those in the family who also remembered it sang with her. As the last note faded, and the twirling fun slowed, Sarah said, "With you, Jesus, all things are possible, all things are blessed. It is your love, Lord, which brings deep and abundant joy. Thank you for all you have given to us today. We love you and honor you."

The whole family rose in unison and serenaded sweetly, almost like an endearing hug,

"Thank you, Lord, for saving my soul,
Thank you, Lord, for making me whole,
Thank you, Lord, for giving to me,
Thy great salvation, so rich and free."

Sarah loved this mountaintop blessing. She knew she would always cherish it. She felt like a little child, not wanting to leave the circus. But this was so much more than a circus event; the blessing of Jesus always grows, compounds, and is multiplied! Every day in His Presence is more blessing, more alive, and more abundant than she experienced even the day before.

As the song floated off in the breeze, Jesus did an "Allemande Left" with all the family, blessing each individually and intimately. Giggling, swooning, and swaying in all that love was the norm in the gazebo that beautiful day.

No one wanted to go, so they moseyed down the mountain together. The ladies carried armfuls of flowers and the men carried the leftovers from their sumptuous lunch. The headiness of the blessing stayed with them; it seemed to Sarah that the flowers released more and more fragrance with every step down the mountainside. Sarah remembered seeing photos of the Jerusalem; the only growth of foliage in them was by irrigation. In the few months since their return from Heaven, the Earth was healing and being restored by its Creator. Everywhere Sarah looked, there was beauty in not only olive trees, but a hundred dazzling varieties of flowers, bushes and trees. She was so very happy she could hardly breathe. How could there be such joy? This is how life was meant to be, living with Jesus right here on this beautiful Earth!

Chapter 15
Pensive Moment with The Spirit

After the blessing on the mountaintop, Sarah padded pensively back to her Holy Land home, savoring the moments with Jesus and her family, as well as the blessing of the birds and the flowers. The setting sun was radiant with golden hues that highlighted everyone and everything with its warm love. For a moment, Sarah paused, realizing that she had never perceived love coming from the sun, but that is exactly what was happening! She quietly asked of the Lord, "My God, does all of nature have emotions?"

The answer came quickly; the Spirit spoke in a gentle, fun tone, for He was amused and blessed by her interest. He said, "Oh my, yes, Little One. All of creation has been given emotion, but only humanity has been given the little item called 'choice'. For nature, the emotions flow out of their natural lives, whether they are hungry or full, curious or needing rest. Emotions in humanity have a dynamic dimension that flows out of not only the natural, but also the choices that are made. Human emotion tends to fluctuate wildly, even moment by moment when action and reaction is in play."

"It's wonderful, Lord!" responded Sarah. "I think this evening was the first time I sensed the love from the sun, as it sends out its rays of light. I felt such joy at the realization!"

"My joy is in the fulfilling your need, as it comes to your awareness, my sweet Little One," affirmed the Spirit. "Anytime you need me, I am here."

Sarah giggled back, "You sure are, everywhere, always, and forever more!" At that she felt a flushing of love enveloping her whole body. What a great answer to her giggling quip!

As she sauntered the last few blocks to her Earth abode, a vision flowed into her head, from a long-ago memory. She was a young teenager, dressed in a lovely pastel dress, which Lila had helped her make. She felt a magical joy, as she twisted colorful ribbons on a May pole with her girlfriends at school. They danced with one lifting her ribbon and another keeping hers down, then switched. The effect was a beautiful pastel ribbon-web. They then turned to undo the interlocked ribbon, then once again dancing and winding into a different pattern intertwining in a beautiful dance of pretty pastels, then releasing the ribbon and dancing on into life. It was an enchanted time in her life; she cherished the memory. She felt the Spirit nudging her just a bit that life with the Lord God was just like that dance, gorgeous, gracious, and glorious. The feelings of joy she had felt when she danced with her friends so long ago in that high school gym were just a hint of the joy she would be experiencing with the Lord and all of her brothers and sisters in Christ.

Sarah felt, with everything in her, that her life would include the intertwining of her life with everyone in the great family of God. It would be a precious dance of God's love, weaving her life in with every person who has been chosen of God and loved by Him from even before creation. It reminded her of the Fibonacci sequence she had learned in school. Beginning with the tiniest effort, the blessings become bigger and bigger, as you continue on. Sarah loved how the truth of God's mathematics is shown in nature; the Fibonacci sequence is all over the place, in the sea shell for just one!

Sarah entered her Earth abode and decided to rest, for a moment, to pray and thank God for the blessings of the mountain, but also of her sweet memory and vision of her joy at the May Pole Dance. She sank into the comfortable lounger and stretched out even her legs to rest her whole body, as she prayed quietly, "Oh my Lord, you have given me so many blessings. I feel so full, like a teapot full to the brim and getting hot, so hot, I'm going to blow in overflowing joy! Stretch me, Lord, so that I will be able to take in more and more of all you pour over me. I'm so full and yet, I'm thirsty for you. You satisfy my every longing and yet, I want more! I know that in you, I am complete; and yet every day I grow more, as an individual and as a part of your great family. If I could spend every moment thanking you for my life in your Presence, it would not be enough. Oh Lord, my God, I rest in you; I breathe in your righteousness, for in me, there is only the righteousness that you have made provision for. I am restored to righteous living because of your love and your willingness to pay the price of my sin, by the shedding of your innocent, pure blood. And because of your grace, I am completely reconciled to you and have this wonderful fellowship with you. What a gift, relationship with God! I feel humbled and yet, you lift me up, give me value, and call me your 'Precious Little One.' How I love you, my Savior and Righteous Brother!" As she finished her prayer, she merely breathed in the breath the Lord provided, acknowledging the gift of life, "Abba, Father, you give me breath; you give me life."

In quiet peace, Sarah tried to stop thinking a moment. It was a new discipline she was trying, closing down her mile-a-minute brain and just stopping the thinking. Often, as she quieted her thoughts, the Holy Spirit would speak to her, whispering to her open mind and heart. Sarah struggled to quiet her thoughts, even focusing on her breathing and slowing that down too. She was not very adept yet, for even focusing on the physical things of the body was a thought process. So she tried to even set that aside and be completely silent....

The Holy Spirit loved that Sarah was doing this exercise in quieting her mind; it revealed her intense dedication to follow God. He was moved and honored and rejoiced so much that He always blessed her. It was not out of duty, or as a payment for her worship, but the blessing of the Spirit was of pure delight in His relationship with His Precious Little One. He poured His love over her, allowing it to seep into all the inner parts of her body, like honey filling up every crevice in a hive. Sarah responded with even more relaxation, of her head, arms and hands; everything went limp in the soaking of God's love.

Then, the whisper of a new endeavor surprised her. "You have been faithful as Jesus' activity assistant. You and Sally have blessed everyone here and honored Jesus with your words and deeds. Generations of new believers have grown in their faith through the activities you and Sally shared so faithfully. Jesus has called another two friends to continue the beautiful ministry you have begun and we have a new work of grace, which will continue to build you up in Christ and bless others as you seek to follow our leading. This is a ministry of larger proportions, as you will be poignantly touching the lives of those who have not yet chosen to receive Christ as their Savior."

Sarah responded in the affirmative, as her heart was broken for those who had refused the Lord, "Oh, my Spirit, I honor you and will endeavor to bless everyone I meet with, that they all may come to receive Christ." A flush of the love of God hit Sarah's body, signaling not only that the Spirit had heard her response, but also cherished it and finally, had left until she needed Him.

Sarah pondered the many blessings she had been given through her activity ministry through Jesus. With every activity, insight and wisdom blessed the individuals participating. Indeed, she remembered men and women, their children, grandchildren, and even great grandchildren, who had grown in faith. They were her friends and her dear brothers and sisters in Christ.

In every generation, there had been individuals who just could not accept that Jesus created the whole universe and was truly God in their midst. Even though Satan was bound, those who were born during this millennial reign of Christ on Earth (born of fallen humanity) still received in their bodies the fallen nature, the tendency toward self-focus. Just the miracle of their birth was pretty wonderful to Sarah. Those who had received the Lord during the Tribulation had not experienced the transformation of their bodies, as the believers who were caught up to Heaven had. They were able to have children and continued to do so for hundreds of years. As new generations grew up, families grew exponentially, with children continuing to bless them. She had noted, though, that as couples lived longer, their bodies began to be transformed; as each couple was ready to let go of having more children, the ability to do so and the interest in sexuality shifted. These mature couples in Christ eventually decided within their relationships, that they were truly more brother and sister in Christ, rather than husband and wife. With this happening at different times for each couple, and the generations overlapping, life on Earth had been very interesting indeed!

Sarah thought back to the first time she had participated with Jesus in reaching out to the skeptical children. She pondered the hardness of their lives, the despair of their broken dreams. Then, her mind drifted to Jesus' invitation to receive His love, their genuine response of faith, and the wonderful joy that filled the whole community of children after they all received Jesus as their Savior. The sweet memory served to encourage her, but also it revealed the reality of what she would be facing in this new ministry.

As Sarah reflected about her new endeavor, she let it soak into her soul, as if she were a sponge, getting bigger and bigger with the love that came seeping in. Even as she felt this love, for the family of God to expand, she also heard the kindhearted voice of the Spirit speak audibly to her, "You are an encourager, compassionate and willing. I will lead you; wherever you go, share with my people spiritual songs of my love."

She replied, feeling awed by the commissioning, "Oh, yes Lord, I will go. I love that you will lead me. I love listening to you, following your direction, and sharing your love with those I meet. Thank you, Lord God, for entrusting to me this superb endeavor." Then, she just started her breathing deep; after a few deep breaths, she added, "Yah," and "weh," as she breathed. She felt the strength and blessing of the Lord permeating within her being when she breathed in the Name of the Lord God.

Sarah glanced around her beautiful Jerusalem abode and thought to herself, "*Ya know, I really do not need to come here every night. I only need a few moments to re-charge throughout the day and night. And – there are so many people who are out and about all night long, I could just be busy with the Lord's commission all the time!*" She decided right then and there to pack a little rucksack with a few things to carry, a Bible, a clean robe to change into, and said to the Lord, "I'm ready, Lord! Guide me and make me a blessing to those whom you love."

Silently, the Spirit impressed upon her mind that she would be moving about within the family of God and reaching out to those who are soon to be a part of the family. She may have very special moments with her own family and even her friends, but there would be much more to this season of her life. She would experience more of worship and outreach to those who needed the particular gifts that God placed into her personality, abundant compassion and gentle encouragement.

Sarah, filled with exuberance and expectation, stepped out into a new expression of her faith.

Chapter 16
Powerful Proclamation in Paint

Sarah didn't have to walk far to begin seeing her family! Mark's Earth abode was directly across from hers. Even though it was just breaking daylight, Mark was already active out in the yard, constructing a platform that would hold his largest painting to date, a huge mural on burnished sheet metal. Everyone loved his paintings so much that he had decided to paint in his front yard, so everyone could comfortably watch him. He had placed some benches scattered in the yard. As Sarah approached, he finished the platform and was ready to put the huge metallic piece, on which he had already painted a latex primer, up onto it. Sarah ran the few steps and lifted one end while Mark lifted the other. They put it in place and then, Mark came over and gave his mom a huge hug. His voice was tender as he thanked his mother, "You are great, Mom. Thanks so much for being here just when I needed you!" (Sarah giggled like a school girl.) "I thought I'd do my work out here; I have so many people who want to watch me paint. I'm starting today on this mural about the joy of living with the Lord. It will be somewhat abstract, but will show his love in waves, flowing over us like an ocean of grace."

Sarah responded, "What a beautiful way to portray the love of God! Do you have a small table for your paints and brushes?"

Mark said, "I sure do; would you like to get it, just inside the front door, while I bring the enamel paint that I will be using out? I've made a palette from an old muffin tin, with space for 12 color shades. It's really nice for painting something large. I can mix the colors together to make even more intricate shades."

Sarah was already moving before her son finished talking. She brought the table out just in time to meet Mark with the muffin tin of paint and a can of brushes. She asked her son, "Would you like to sit a moment and have some juice before you begin to paint?"

"Sure!" Mark replied. "It's very good to rest a moment and pray before painting. With the Lord, I am so quickly inspired that my hands almost fly, with the paint taking on a life of its own!" He grabbed his mother's hand and brought it to his chest. "Mom, I am so blessed to do this! I can hardly contain the joy. I have some juice inside; I'll go get it and we can sit in the cool beauty of the morning." He released her hand and went inside.

Sarah lifted her eyes and hands to Heaven and tenderly thanked God for her son. Then she turned and walked toward one of the long benches, which were hewn from local trees, sanded and protected with clear varnish that highlighted the natural beauty of the wood. She sat down, running her hand over the smooth surface. When she looked up, Mark handed her a glass and she smiled broadly and sipped the luscious nectar.

Mark sat next to her and slurped his nectar like he was a guy lost in a desert. At length, he said, "I sure like this! I can't get enough! It's my favorite; even though we need less to keep our bodies going, there's no adverse effects of enjoying eating and drinking so many delectable delights, like that terrible weight gain. I was so tired of being called 'Supersize' when I was so chubby, I could almost roll around instead of walking!"

Sarah laughed, throwing her head back, with her long loosely curled hair joining the fun. Indeed, she remembered his rotund shape of so long ago, so utterly different from the healthy, even buff guy sitting with her now. She affirmed, "It is great, so refreshing!" Then, in a more pensive voice, Sarah asked Mark, "Son, what would you say is the most important thing about life here, back on Earth once again?"

Mark bent his head and closed his eyes in quiet meditation for a moment, then replied, "I think that knowing Jesus in this very personal relationship is the most invaluable, profound experience in all of life. I have never been more at peace, more grounded, and more challenged to reflect His glory." With that, he smiled and hugged his mother fiercely and tenderly.

Sarah's eyes abounded with tears of joy and love. (She never had tears of sadness or sorrow anymore.) She breathed in deep and agreed, "It's the best, being with Jesus in such an intense way. I really love experiencing Him through His Spirit, who is ever with us! You have a beautiful gift, son. Your paintings are all over Jerusalem and even out in the surrounding neighborhoods. They are blessing people, with the beauty of color and design that you put in each painting."

"Thank you, Mom. I think perhaps I needed you this morning, to encourage me to continue on! I love painting and once I get started, it flows so easily. I know the Spirit is inspiring me and blessing people through the paintings. You are so precious to me, Mom; you gave me life, along with the Lord, of course, and raised me. You have known all my foibles and the profound way the Lord blessed me in my young adult years. And now, we are so much more than mother and son. It is like an extra dimension of life, a fourth dimension, one of everlasting life and immeasurable joy. The fact that I am your son is only the beginning of who we are and how we experience life together. I think that perhaps that is the deeper significance of your visit. Once again, God is working through you to bring me closer in relationship with Him and you too, likewise, with every one of my brothers and sisters in Christ. Thank you, Mom; I love you so."

Sarah sighed deeply and allowed herself to be swallowed up in his embrace. She looked up to his wide smile and gave him a grin that blessed him all the more. They both bowed their heads, her diminutive hand resting in his broad palm. Sarah led their prayer, "Oh Lord God, we are so thankful to be yours. We trust you completely with our lives. As we join together, mother and son, we seek your direction for our every step, every brushstroke in the glorious colors you have created. You have blessed us with abilities; we commit all that we are to reflect your glory. Be with us in a unique way today and every day, Lord, and help us to see, feel, and internalize the love you have for us. We ask these things in your name, oh Jesus, our Savior and Lord."

Mark joined his mother, as they both said, "Amen" with a depth of emotion that seemed more profound than either had experienced before. "Oh Mom, I felt such a surge of blessings over me; it is as though the Lord poured His love over me like a waterfall. I think He also gave me insight for my painting, the direction I need to go and how to express it. Wow, I feel so invigorated!" With that, he jumped up and began filling his muffin tin painting palette.

Sarah felt the same rejuvenation; she arose with a shivering of her whole body, a the Spirit confirmed His blessings upon her and her head, laughed enthusiastically, rejoicing in the goodness of God. She felt the sun beginning to warm her shoulders, a mere fraction of the love of God that blazed within her. She relaxed and watched, as Mark began to make broad strokes of color on the metallic surface. As she watched the form and color of his painting build, Sarah was truly in awe of the capability God had placed in him, to co-create such inspiring paintings. Neighbors and friends drifted in, sitting on the benches, standing behind them, and even more sitting in front of them. All around were whispers and "ahhh's" of the beauty he was painting. As the crowd grew, the awe grew. Great, sweeping, white-capped waves pommeled the sandy shore. It was as though every person could feel the power of God's love pouring over them, enveloping them in a love so complete that its depths could not be fathomed.

Just as Mark finished the masterpiece, Jesus walked up to him from far back in the crowd and embraced him in a macho, side hug. He exclaimed, "Beautiful, Mark! Even I am mesmerized by the power of this painting. It captures very well the power of the love of our Father, myself and our Spirit. You have been faithful to utilize the ability we have placed in you, to bless all of the family of God. When this dries, may I hang it above the entry of the Community Center?"

Mark replied, "Oh yes, I would be delighted if you would. I'll bring it over this evening." With that, Mark bowed low and acknowledged, "It is by your grace that I am able to paint at all. I love to explore every aspect of life in You with art. Thank you, Jesus, for the love you pour over us!" He then sat down where he was, for there was no other space. The attention of the people shifted from the artist to the Creator of all.

Jesus addressed the huge gathering in Mark's front lawn, speaking eloquently of the love of the Triune God, "Our love is indeed like the ocean waves. It comes with power and fulfilment, wrapping all of humanity in inexpressible wellbeing. We give our love, in increasing intensity, as each individual is able to receive it. I bless you today, with just a tiny ripple of that love." Jesus lifted His arms and moved his hands lightly toward the audience. The wave of love was so intense that every person was propelled backwards and they each laid back, many on the laps of those behind them. There were no problems because everyone was only aware of this great and powerful love, rather than what was happening to them physically. Jesus lifted His arms toward Father God; they united in the full power of their Holy love.

After quite a while of just resting and receiving the love Jesus poured over them, people began to stir, sitting up or standing as they had before. Conversations erupted with enthusiasm. Amid the bustling activity, Sarah and Mark found each other and embraced, both enraptured by all they had just experienced. Sarah whispered into her son's ear, "Thank you so much, Mark, for your faithfulness to the Lord and to your talent. I'm going to take a walk for now. God bless you, my son. I love you so…"

"Love you too, Mom," Mark whispered back with emotion. "Have a wonderful day!" He released her and with a loving glance in each other's eyes, Sarah meandered through the crowd toward the side yard and on toward a path that encircles the neighborhood.

Even though Jesus was quite occupied with so many who shared their joy with Him and honored Him, when He noticed Sarah, He quickly and graciously ended His current conversation. Jesus pursued Sarah and drew her attention just as she was turning onto the path. He gently said her name and she gasped and turned toward Him, feeling the fullness of His love and the wonder that He wanted to talk with her.

He began, with tenderness and love enveloping every word, "I want to give you another, more personal blessing. You have received the gift of encouragement, and now you are willing to explore utilizing that gift even more. There is a tenderness about you that was born out of the suffering and the healing of it; as I bring you to individuals, know that this gift is exactly what they need." He drew her into a sweet embrace and held her head and shoulders in his hands. He declared over her, "Sarah, you are the embodiment of my love. As you speak and touch my family, you are blessed in even more of this precious gift. Tenderness will ooze out of you like a water balloon with holes, but it will never leave you completely. It will be a constant replenished blessing for everyone, but also and especially for you."

Sarah could only respond in gratitude, "Oh Lord, thank you for all of this. I feel so blessed; I can hardly contain it all!" She looked up into His deep, intensely loving eyes and felt as though she was completely melting, like a puddle of butter. When He released her, she regained her balance and smiled broadly, saying, "You are my source, my Lord. With all that I am, I honor you."

Jesus affirmed to His precious Sarah, "I created you for many things. One aim is that you would display my glory before many; you do so charmingly. Go with my peace and love."

Sarah replied, "I will, my Lord!" She watched Jesus, as He turned back to bless more people who were still marveling at the power of the love of God. He was quickly enveloped in a group of joyful men and women.

Sarah felt like her body would burst with the fullness of health, blessing, and utter delight. She had no need, as she stretched out her legs on the morning walk, but was ready for whatever the Lord guided her to. She thought for a moment, *"How different this is from working every day to get money, to buy stuff, and fall into bed at night, exhausted and depressed! With Jesus, my every necessity is provided for, my every desire opens up new blessings and new joy with God."* She had no concept of what experience may be just around the bend; nevertheless, Sarah held anticipation in her soul like a sturdy walking stick. With each new day, she learned more about living a life of faith and rejoiced in the entire process.

Chapter 17
New Path of Blessing

Along the path, Sarah came to another path that she had not taken before. Always the explorer, she did not hesitate when she felt the prompting of the Spirit to follow it. She found this to be a manicured path, lined with tulips, daffodils, hyacinths, and a myriad of floral varieties she was not familiar with. Bright, beautiful colors and sweet fragrances filled the morning with a heady feeling, identical to how she felt the first time she walked in Heaven's Gardens. As she rounded a curve in the path, the flowers gave way to blossoming shrubs, azaleas, roses, and primroses. Sarah felt her senses heighten; she felt as though she was given a hint of the spiritual blessing ahead, with bigger and more flowers, bigger plants, and even greater headiness. She wanted to slow down and experience every aspect of this. At the same time, she wanted to go faster, to arrive at the fullness of God's blessing!

Sarah forced herself to slowly meander down the path and enjoy every moment of all that the Lord had arranged. A bit further down the path held another corner tightly it its grip. Sarah took the turn with her head surveying high and low the gorgeous foliage. The exclamation, "Oh my!" escaped her lips when the path ushered into a huge, oval floral room. The rhododendron, hydrangeas, hollyhocks, and butterfly bushes were simply luscious in their regal floral display, which dwarfed Sarah by at least several feet in height. Numerous invitingly-adorned loungers had been arranged in a smaller oval; some were even rockers. Sarah loved rockers and sank into one, relaxing her head back and her feet up, to revel in the loveliness surrounding her.

Sarah once again began praising the Lord God, thanking Him for the beauty of this place. She began to sense she was not alone in her worship of her Lord. At first, she heard only a hum, very quietly. The hum grew in depth, with more voices joining in. A beautiful harmony developed, with deep voices of the thicker, heavier plants, all the way up the scale to the tiny delicate vines that crept around and up, balancing on the branches of the succulent bushes of the floral room. They emitted the most beautiful, clear tones; it sounded like the light whistling of a piccolo to Sarah. She began to sing, with all the flowering foliage following her lead,

"This is my Father's world,
and to my listening ears all nature sings,
and round me rings the music of the spheres.

This is my Father's world:
I rest me in the thought
of rocks and trees, of skies and seas;
his hand the wonders wrought."

When Sarah finished the song, she timidly stopped, to listen to nature itself singing God's praises. There was an anthem that rose, almost like the "Halleluiah Chorus" from Handel's "Messiah." The entire range of glorious tones, from even deeper than the bass's all the way up beyond the soprano's piercing high notes, lifted their praises to the Lord God. Sarah laid back, transfixed by the hymn of nature. Sarah learned that morning, of the real beauty of nature - its songs to the Lord.

At length, the flowering foliage began to lessen their powerful worship and slowly took it down to a melodious hum. Sarah just rested in a tender worship of her Lord, thanking Him for the beauty of this place and the joy of His Presence in her life.

The Spirit whispered to her, "My sweet Sarah, it is our pleasure to be in relationship with you. Blessings flow, from your heart to us and from ours to you. We love you ever more."

Sarah received the blessing with a renewed "Thank you" in her heart. She pondered this beautiful garden and her experience here and remembered long ago, when she was just a girl in a high school choir. They sang an arrangement of "The Road Less Traveled" by Robert Frost, which ended with:

> "I shall be telling this with a sigh
> Somewhere ages and ages hence:
> Two roads diverged in a wood, and I—
> I took the one less traveled by,
> And that has made all the difference"

Sarah remembered the beautiful melody and marveled at how fitting it was for her, this morning, in this place. As she lay back and soaked in the beauty, she just listened, trying not to think, just listen. She once again entered into the discipline that she had been recently developing, quieting her thoughts to listen to whatever was present, whether it was a thundering downpour, or twittering birds, or perhaps the Lord imparting new blessings to her heart, mind, and soul.

It began with a feeling, of great tenderness toward her. She sensed the Holy Spirit with her in a new way. Tingling began to envelope her entire body with a love so profound that she fell completely limp in the lounger. The Presence of the Spirit seemed to make the air thick with love, like a hot, humid sauna. Sarah felt a profound aspect of being known by the Spirit. It was more intimate than she had ever experienced; she had no fear, but instead felt like she could hardly breathe with the power of this love upon her. Her body functioned; she did breathe! But oh, the joy of this moment! She knew that she could stay in complete, intimate fellowship with The Spirit as long as she wanted. She was so very blessed that she just rested in His love for the longest time.

Without any concept of time passing, Sarah relished this great intimacy with the God who created her and loved her. Divine love was so far above her in dimension and power; she could only receive it. She felt it permeate every part of her body, rejuvenating every cell even more than before. As she thought of it, she didn't even understand how that could be, but accepted it as absolute truth. She began to perceive more about what she had experienced.

The first thought that came to mind was that rejecting something does not make it untrue. It simply means that the one rejecting it will not experience the fullness of its truth. Sarah thought of a funny way to express it. If a fella sees a chair, but does not believe anything about the chair's strength and durability to hold his weight, he would not sit in it because of his strong doubt. No matter how many people tell him that the chair will hold him without breaking, he adamantly refuses to believe so. He refuses to sit, even if he is sore from standing too long. His fear of falling overrides any interest he would even have of trying the chair out. He does not experience the truth of the strength of that chair, but his unbelief does not diminish in any way the strength of the chair. He never experiences the relaxing rest the chair offers. The chair does not have to convince him in order to have the intrinsic truth of its existence. It is there for him if he wants to have faith in its strength. In addition, his unbelief never diminishes the faithfulness of the chair; it remains available to him if he finds that he is willing to step beyond his doubt and into a new level of faith.

"*Wow!*" Sarah mused, "*I've never thought through faith in this way; it seems so simple when breaking it down in steps. People who choose unbelief in Jesus Christ in no way diminishes Him; they just do not experience the truth of His power and love.*" She was so thankful she had chosen faith! The blessings continued to roll over her like the tiny blossoms that had been released from the fruit trees and rolled around on the wind, ever more beautiful and fragrant.

Another illuminating thought poked its head over the edge of her brain. *"Without the choice of receiving the gift of love the Lord Jesus offers all of humanity, there is only bleak, everlasting horror that is devoid of God, His love, and His provision."* She had experienced an ever-increasing level of joy and fulfillment with Jesus in her life. Sarah began to realize that the inverse is true also; without Him, there is an ever-increasing sense of foreboding, physical and emotional pain, and profound loss.

In that moment of renewed understanding, Sarah was ever-so-thankful that the Lord still allowed this freedom of thought. She realized that the ability to think through these positive and negative aspects of eternal life was extremely important. It served not only to reinforce her personal decision to entrust her life to the loving hands of her Savior, Jesus Christ, but also to encourage others to do so as well.. *"How wonderful it is that He is here!"* she affirmed to herself softly, in complete awe..

With a deep breath of the heady fragrance, Sarah stood up and leaned her head back, stretching her back and inwardly, her heart - to be open to all the grace of the Lord Jesus in her life. She turned, without a thought in her head about the path ahead, only thinking of her Lord. A fun, light song from her youth popped into her head and she sang the sweet tune, as she sauntered back down the path,

> "Oh, Happy Day, Oh Happy Day,
> When Jesus washed,
> He washed my sins away,
> Oh, Happy Day!"

Chapter 18
Meandering in the Spirit

Sarah felt light and carefree; she was filled beyond measure and stretched out her legs in a brisk walk. She had rejoined the main path and felt so invigorated that she savored every flower, bush, and tree she could see. Breathing deep, Sarah twirled around and lifted her eyes and hands toward the clear, blue sky, praising God. She just twirled in place, expressing her joy to the Lord, even closing her eyes to more intensely focus on the power and Presence of the Lord.

When at last Sarah felt released from her passionate worship, she came back to focus on the trail and the direction she was headed. Feeling a prompting from the Spirit, she glanced back toward the worship garden path from whence she came and saw a dear friend come sauntering around the corner and into view. "Oh my", Sarah thought, *"How wonderful! I have not seen Sweeny since before the terrible car accident that rendered her body mangled, a few years before Resurrection Morning!"* When their eyes met, their faces lit up like the sunrise, with huge smiles and eyes twinkling with joy. They both ran the short distance between each other and embraced tenderly.

Sweeny spoke first, "I have missed you so much, Sarah. My departure from Earth was so abrupt, but oh, how happy I have been being with Jesus! My body no longer hurts; I love this new body I've been given! I'm no longer limited by the rotten bone disorder that left my limbs short and in pain; I can stretch out my legs and run now!" Indeed, she was quite a bit taller than she had been. "I know the car accident was hard for you to experience the aftermath of, but Jesus knew the number of my days! I didn't suffer in pain; He lifted my spirit right out of that pain-wracked body and now I am the person He created me to be – and oh, so happy for the transformation! I'm surprised we didn't run into each other up in Heaven; but then, there are so many believers, from all generations of humanity. This morning, I felt the Spirit nudge me a bit, and this beautiful path came to mind. I ate a bit and roamed the path, enjoying the greater beauty of the Earth. Jesus has healed so many things and has given nourishment in abundance for all living things." Sweeny reached for her friend's hand and holding it tightly to her chest, whispered, "You are so precious to me, Sarah." With that, they hugged again, with tender hearts.

Sarah responded, her voice a bit tight with emotion, "Yes, I missed you. I knew your spirit was with the Lord, but I missed you so much! I felt like I couldn't breathe, my grief was so deep. I knew your body was so broken that you would not want to be tethered to it. And look at you now, the picture of our eternal health in Christ! Your beauty shines even more now, for it is no longer lessened even a smidgen by old Satan. You are even more the bouncy, affectionate, and fun gal with gorgeous brunette hair bobbed to match your bubbly personality! I remember how much I enjoyed the very special fellowship you and I had; it was like a an indestructible bond had been forged between us because of the crucible of childhood abuse. We understood each other's pain and shared the empathy and compassion of Christ that is possible nowhere else." With a tender hug, Sarah asked, "Will you join me? We can stroll the path together!"

"I'd love to," Sweeny replied. "We have so much to catch up on. You know, back on Earth, I really thought of you as my mother, even though you were to be my mother-in-law. You provided the spiritual and personal encouragement that I so needed. Yes, there was a special connection in Christ, which so powerfully bonded us together. I think it was that we had both suffered so much and that Christ has a special, deep level of compassion for little ones who suffer. And now, we have eternity to have this great relationship grow and develop beyond anything we could ever imagine. Oh, Sarah, thank you for all you have given to me."

Sarah felt like she had been blessed clear to her toes. She affirmed to Sweeny, "Oh, thank you; I have been so invigorated by your sweet smile, your effervescent personality, and the fellowship that we had and now, have again. I realized only after you had gone, and I was left waiting for that glorious Resurrection Morning, that I had opened my heart so much that I thought of you as my daughter and cherished you with all that is in me. My, I think the Lord prepared this morning for our reunion, for our blessing today and forever!"

"I agree," Sweeny quipped, "but there is something more to it. Jesus is blessing us, so that we can bless even more people. Let's sit here a moment and pray," Sweeny said, indicating a wooden bench, whose slats were contoured for comfort. The two ladies sat together, and clasping together their four hands, united in prayer before the Lord Jesus. Sweeny began, "Oh, Lord Jesus, thank you for all you have done for us, for our salvation and fellowship with each other. Thank you for that bond of mother/daughter love and care that we had for each other and now for this great sister relationship that pulses within the tender hearts you have given us. We ask you, Lord, for guidance and direction, for how you would like us to proceed, to give you honor and glory."

Sarah continued, "Yes, Lord Jesus, reveal to us the next step. And help us to listen well to your prompting and to go forth in confidence to the direction you would like us to take. Thank you for my dear friend Sweeny, and for our continuing and growing fellowship. Be with us, Lord, as we walk this beautiful path, ever lifting up praise to you, Jesus." They sat in expectant silence for a long while, listening, then together had come to the end and both whispered, "Amen."

Sweeny shared, "I felt the Lord saying, 'Come with me down this path. Come and dance!' That sounds wonderful; let's go!" The two gals held hands and skipped down the lane, in a joyful, playful meandering in the beautiful, Mediterranean woodland. Soon they began to hear just a whispering of an uplifting tune, which became a lovely sonata as they drew closer. Sarah and Sweeny slowed to a brisk walk, listening intently as they approached the burgeoning symphony that supported the singers. In the distance, they saw the forested path give way to a meadow, with luscious grass dotted with a rainbow of flowers. The closer they came, the more beautiful the music resounded.

Sarah caught her breath when they finally stepped from the forest and into the broad meadow. The orchestra and choir were in the center of the great space, with line dancers surrounding them in ever-growing rings. The music swelled and flew around the meadow like it had wings of its own. She was mesmerized by the music, so much that she didn't notice Sweeny dashing ahead of her to join in with the line dancers. The symphony was so beautiful; Sarah felt lifted above the Earth and began dancing in the sky - her arms waved and circled in perfect time with the tympani drums. They carried the foundation of the tempo, solid and grand, from which the entire orchestra flowed its gorgeous harmony. She laughed and danced and sang praises to God, adding to the thousands who were similarly enraptured.

Sarah noticed Sweeny up in the air, dancing and flying too, with a song of Jesus whirling about her, "I am trusting in you, Jesus! You are above everything in the Earth, I am flying in my joy over you!" She sang even louder, "Oh Lord Jesus, I love you! I love flying! Thank you! I praise your Name!"

Sarah asked the Spirit to reveal all the spiritual dimension of all that was happening there. In hardly a moment, her eyes and ears popped a bit with the shift, which revealed the sky above full of angels praising the Lord and blessing everyone gathered in the meadow, with the love of God that radiated from their glistening wings.

Sarah felt herself buoyed even more with the blessings from the angels and embraced the worship of their Savior. The angels flew in a large ring, hovering some 100 feet above the orchestra laden meadow. In doing so, a wind tunnel formed, drawing the worshippers up higher and toward the center. More and more people were coming from many trails, into the meadow. The meadow was replete with dancers worshipping in cadence with the symphonic orchestra. The air above meadow teemed with layers of humanity dancing, singing, and in all, worshipping. Sarah felt exhilarated; she loved experiencing all of the blessings the Lord continually brought into her life.

Sarah noticed some of those above her conveying their praises out of their mouths and hands so copiously, they fell backward in the air and into a back flip, coming back up to praise again. They were so blessed, more and more worshippers joined in with each flip. "Oh, yes," Sarah thought, "I need to do this!" She watched for a moment and then sent out her praise to the Lord, "You are the Almighty, the Everlasting Lord!" The power of her worship and the blessing of the Spirit rolled her backward and into the flip. Sarah came back up laughing so hard she bumped into a couple of kids that were chortling in the sheer fun of worship. A few more praise-initiated back flips and Sarah began to feel like she would explode in manifest acclamation of the Lord Jesus.

The angels flew in a huge loop of splendidness around the entire meadow. Orchestral melodies and harmonies billowed upward from the master choir musicians far below. Line dancers danced independently - but in unison, in fourteen ever-expanding rings encircling the orchestra. They twirled, jumped, and swayed, with their arms and hands ever moving in praise of the Lord. With all those worshipping with Sarah in the air, she thought, "*It reminds me of the ripples in the water, expanding into ever-widening circles.*" The worship of the Living Lord was palpable; it was like losing oneself in the absolute completeness of the Triune God. Sarah felt more blessed in the midst of this worship than ever before in all her life. For the briefest of moments, she wondered how it was even possible to experience more and more blessing and deeper and more powerful worship as time went on.

Even as she was pondering all of this, way up in the air, the enriching words of the Spirit spoke to her spirit, "Ah, my sweetness, with all of eternity stretching out before you – with no end at all, there will always be growth, expansion, more blessing to experience, and deeper, more profound worship. We will bless you and challenge you to strive for the utmost that we have for you. You, in turn, will bless many with the unique gifts we have placed in you. So, have fun in worship; be blessed in the power of the Name of God. Look, coming to receive the honor that is being given here, is the Savior…"

Sarah looked up and watched Jesus descending from the clouds, much like He had done on Resurrection Morning. (that glorious day!) With Him were a myriad of glorious angels, flying all around Him, in every direction and yet, Sarah observed, not ever flying into each other! It was such a beautiful sight; everyone in the meadow and in the air above it, stopped in awe. Sarah did not even have to think about staying afloat in the air; her worship buoyed her up – it was the power of faith intertwined with the power of Jesus in such a tight connection, nothing else was needed. The angels who had encircled the worshippers, flew up and joined the other angels, uniting with them in worship of the King of kings.

Jesus wore royal robes of fine linen, adorned with precious gems and chains of pure gold, the High Priest for all of humanity. As He slowly descended, those in the air followed Him, drawing closer to Him as they also descended. Sarah felt the beckoning of His Spirit; she wanted to follow even more closely, but was compassionate and polite to all the others who were gathering close to Him. Jesus descended upon the meadow just to one side of the orchestra; immediately all of humanity fell to their knees and some, fully prostrate before their Lord.

Sarah felt her whole body go limp before the power of The Lord. At the very same time, His compassion and absolute love flooded her, and in no more than a moment, she landed, more on her nose than anything else! She felt no pain, but her body just eased into the landing amid her sense of utter humility in the Presence of the Creator and Sustainer of her faith. It was the first time she had ever experienced His Presence as her High Priest; she felt so small and insignificant in the Presence of His utter Holiness. She wanted to sing her worship of Him, but could only sing out in tone, not in word. Her worship mingled with a myriad of similar songs sung without a word, lifting above in great beauty.

Jesus lifted up His arms and spoke of His love for every person in that beautiful meadow. She heard the Spirit confirm not only the love of the Triune God for her, but also that the expression of love was personal and intimate for each person.

Chapter 19
Pockets of Discomfort

AS Sarah relaxed after the intense worship experience, she began to feel the depth of Jesus love for those who had not yet received Him. The Spirit affirmed that this was just a hint of the profound love of God; it would overwhelm her if it were all revealed. Indeed, Sarah felt as if love had consumed her in every way possible. She stood and made her way to Sweeny, to share her heart and the new direction in which she felt the Spirit guiding her.

Sweeny was rolling around on the beautiful flowers, giggling as the Lord blessed her. The giggles subsided and she smiled and lifted her head. Sarah bent down and took her hand to lift her up, then gave her a tender hug. They strolled toward the orchestra and shared their joy of the dancing and worship.

Presently, Sarah shared her heart for following the commissioning of Jesus to the not-yet-believers, "Sweeny, the Lord is guiding me to visit the numerous groups of not-yet-believers, to share His love and encourage them to receive Him. I think the time is now, for me to embark on the journey."

"Oh my," Sweeny jumped in, "I have been praying for someone to go with me to the not-yet-believers. My heart has been burdened for a long time, for their personal suffering and their eternal life choice. So often, people do not realize that when they do not actively choose to follow the Lord Jesus, they are actually rejecting Him from their lives and that is an eternal choice. We still have time to encourage them to consider a life of love and peace, rather than suffering and pain. How about if we go together?"

Sarah replied, "Yes, I am honored to go with you, Sweeny. Let's stop and pray for the journey."

The ladies paused right where they were and knelt on the blanket of floral abundance. Sweeny launched into a heartfelt prayer of dedication, "Lord Jesus, we ask that you would bless our efforts and bring miraculous waves of your love that will flow over those who are not yet decided about their eternal destination. May it always be you, Lord, whom they choose to follow. We stand united in our purpose to glorify you. Bless us, our Lord Jesus."

As the last word of Sweeny's prayer was spoken, a visible, shimmery blanket of love and peace spread over both Sarah and Sweeny and the voice of the Spirit spoke audibly in the meadow, "You will go with the blessing of God upon your words and actions. This blanket of love and peace will be a symbol of the truth of your message. And, your angels will accompany you, to protect you and provide for your needs in every situation. Every heart which is open to the message of Jesus' love will receive and be eternally saved. Be blessed, my Little Ones."

Sarah and Sweeny hugged; as they released each other, they were surrounded by many who had heard the blessing of the Spirit upon their journey and received many hugs and blessings. Paul swung Sarah around and squeezed his dear one in a passionate hug, whispering blessings to her. And Sweeny was caught up in a girl hug, from sisters whom she had encouraged back in Heaven, and here on Earth.

When they were released, a path of golden sparkles flashed on the grass and flowers. Sweeny exclaimed, "Jesus has even given us a path to follow!" Everyone laughed and waved, as the two ladies set off, with their angels, Keturael and Abdiel, one before and one after them, covering them in protection and love.

Entering into the forest from a different path than they entered, Sweeny followed her beautiful angel, Abdiel with an excitement building within her. It felt to her like it was a boiling volcano of God's purpose for her life, which was about to burst and come forth with the most blessed of hot, steaming lava of Jesus' love and flow all over all who stand and seek His name.

Sarah felt doubly blessed, for not only was she following the guidance directly from the Spirit, but she was also helping her friend, with the deepest of her longings. The forest surrounded them with a profound beauty, with vibrant colors and gorgeous shrubs, towering trees, and flowers in every nook and cranny available, it seemed. She breathed in the heady, evergreen smells and felt the blessings of complete body health and profound emotional health that lifted joy to the level of ecstasy. She felt no fear, but instead existed in the comprehensive peace of knowing the Creator.

Their walk was of purpose, so it was more than a meandering among the beauties of the forest. After quite a little bit, Sarah began to be aware of the first pocket of discomfort. She could sense tendrils of discontent floating in the morning breeze through the boughs of the evergreens. Soon, it became an acrid smell, uncomfortable to her nose and unnerving to her sensibilities. She breathed a prayer of consecration, "Jesus, be with us in a very special way, as we enter in this more intense area of serving you. Thank you for this precious blanket of love that you have covered over us and for the wondrous protection of our glorious angels."

Sweeny also felt the uptick in intensity; however, she had been so prepared for this ministry that she took it in stride. In fact, the intensity merely strengthened her resolve to follow the leading of the Lord. She joined with Sarah in her prayer, but her heart was singing praises at what the Lord was doing in and through the two ladies. She could hardly keep the lid on her excitement and anticipation of all that the Lord had prepared for them to do.

As they rounded a corner in the forest path, a small group of huts almost hid themselves in a thicket of smaller trees amongst the older-growth trees. Sarah was surprised at the beauty of tender cared-for florals highlighting the paths; she had half-expected a run-down mess filled with miserable inhabitants. What greeted her was a group of happy people doing well in their solitary lives. But the discord was intense, palpable in a strange way. It felt like everything on the surface was so very much at ease, comfortable, and happy; yet, there was a tightness, like a mistaken bubble had popped and oozed-out misery.

The people sensed something different in their midst and came out to investigate. They came from every angle and soon, the small group was encircled with confused, smiling people. No one knew how to address the other; Sweeny and Sarah didn't quite comprehend the juxtaposition of these seemingly contented, yet spiritually miserable individuals. And they seemed just as confused by the appearance of two ladies, in whom they sensed an unknown sense of peace and the two angels who accompanied them, full of beauty and power. Setting aside her muddled-mind, Sarah jumped in, "Hello, we have come to share with you the joy that following Jesus has brought to our lives. We know that you have full autonomy and you have done beautifully here. I'm Sarah and my friend here is Sweeny; we are taking a walk today, sharing our love and how Jesus has transformed our lives. Can we offer you some Heavenly Delights, as we learned to call them in Heaven?" For indeed, the angels had turned to the side and lifted off the strong branches of a broad evergreen a huge tray of the decadent, chocolate sweets, the first of many miraculous blessings that would accompany them.

The circle of faces lightened up with the prospect of a sweet desert and they led the visitors to their communal eating circle. As everyone sat, Sarah and Sally served the deserts. Sweeny began her presentation of God's love and care for her, even in her childhood - in the midst of tremendous abuse and violence. She affirmed, "I grew up in the season of the First Earth, when violence was rampant.

Every day, I endured begin beaten and even my body was used – against my will, for the pleasure of the ones who used me." She looked over the group, who had sad, quizzical looks on their faces, and explained more fully, "Satan had full reign on the Earth at that time and his influence was felt in every home and in every city. The discord was more than just spiritual; it was physical and caused tremendous physical suffering. Way too often, that came in the form of sexual assault, which is what I was forced to endure many times. My own suffering brought me to a place that I realized that I needed God in my life every moment of every day. In a sense, I came to the end of myself, realizing that I had no personal power to take care of myself. I chose to ask Jesus to be my Savior and He began the healing of my heart immediately. He brought joy and peace and even then, within a society that glorified violence, I experienced great healing and joy. Living with Jesus now, in Second Earth, there is the most wonderful joy that fills my heart every day. What is really surprising to me is that the joy continues to grow every day and somehow, my heart and mind expand with it. Sometimes, I feel like I'm going to explode with all of it, but it feels so absolutely wonderful, I never do!"

One of the young lads raised his hand and Sweeny nodded, so he asked the question that burned in his heart, "How is it that we seem happy, we live a life of peace, and have no violence here, and yet, there is a longing that is never fulfilled, not with food, or friend, family, or even physical pleasure?"

Sweeny answered gently, "We are living in a wonderful season of life on Earth. Jesus has bound Satan and his influence for a thousand years and you have the benefit of that. Hatred and anger no longer reign, but that soul hunger is something deeper. It is a hunger for God, for a relationship with the One who created all things. Jesus holds everything in its place and longs for relationship with each and every person. He is the perfect gentleman; He offers wonders beyond our imagination and deep, profoundly fulfilling relationship with us, but patiently waits for our choice to be made. He will not force you to be in relationship with Him, but will bless you beyond all that you could even conceive of, should you choose to enter into relationship with Him. In fact, He has said, 'Wherever two or more are gathered in my Name, there I am in the midst of them.'"

As she finished the last word, Jesus stepped into the circle. There was no mistaking who He was or that He was who He claimed to be. Everyone sat in rapt, stunned silence. His words softened their hearts and minds; Sarah and Sweeny witnessed their visage shift from discord and confusion to peace and joy. He spoke over them, "Perhaps when you were young, in a childlike moment of rebellion, you stepped aside to live in this solitary place. You have been always in my heart, every one of you." He paused, taking time to look into the eyes of every face; His gaze brought peace and love to their souls. They could not ignore His behest, "I love you and long to be with you, but only if you choose to be with me too. Forced relationship is no relationship at all. What do you think, my dear ones?"

From the youngest to the oldest, there was a rippling of movement, from those sitting to standing and reaching out to Jesus for their first moment of true fellowship, with the Lord Jesus.

Sarah and Sweeny and their angels visited dozens of disheveled divots of people, downtrodden and disenfranchised by their own choices. In each, sweet refreshments and hope were given in abundance; Jesus fulfilled every need in His appearance before the people He loved. And they received Him and His offer of love, peace, joy, and eternal relationship. It was a labor of love, not counted by number, days or nights, or even years. Each of the ladies brought their own story of needing Jesus, receiving Him, and the difference that made in their lives. They did not denigrate, belittle, or poke fun at anyone, but encouraged people by listening, sharing, and serving them. Sarah felt entirely blessed, just to share her love of Jesus and her life-transforming relationship with Him. The personal connection with individuals who were confused, questioning, and ultimately, seeking God (even if they didn't realize it) proved to be the turning point for many. Then, when Jesus came to be with each group, and opened His love in an intimate way to them, their confusion melted away. Longing that had nagged them like old weeds withered and faith flourished like blossoming flowers into their hearts and lives.

As the last group of people were enfolded into God's faithful family, Sarah and Sweeny, felt the tender arms of Jesus enfold them both. He spoke over them sweet words of love and appreciation, "Sarah and Sweeny, you both have blessed so many, easing their confusion and helping to prepare them for this life of faith. I honor the time, energy, and tenderness that you so freely have given." He placed upon their shoulders exquisite, intricately laced shawls of blue, gold, and shimmery teal. "These are to bless you for your faithfulness and be a reminder of my intense love for you both."

Sarah lightly touched the beautiful shawl and tying the ends into a loose knot, leaned her head on His chest and hugged Him, honoring her Lord in her heart when words could not express all that she held inside. Sweeny received hers in awe, tied it loosely, and looked up into the eyes of her Lord, melting in His love. Her body became limp in her awe-struck joy. He held her close and at the same time, received the worship of her heart. Time held no limit upon the ones offering love and worship, nor the Creator of time itself, who in receiving love and worship, merely radiated out more of Himself to these whom He had created, especially for this precious relationship of love.

Feeling a bit spent, Sarah lifted her head from Jesus' chest and smiled the biggest, happiest smile – it was almost like her entire face smiled! Her eyes sparkled, her cheeks flushed, and then she laughed. It started with a giggle, but soon, she broke out in an all-out guffaw! Sweeny and Jesus joined in and they laughed until they were all rolling on the grassy carpet beneath them.

After quite a while of all-out snickering, the three unruffled themselves and stood up once again. Jesus grabbed the gals' hands and offered, "Would you like to attend with me a very large celebration? It is being prepared right now and if we zip over there, we'll be right on time!"

Sarah and Sweeny jumped up and down, as if they were little girls, chiming in together, "Oh yes, we would love to." Even as they finished the last word, Jesus whisked them off to the celebration, a Feast for the Faithful.

Chapter 20
A Feast for the Faithful

Sarah was a bit unsteady when she arrived, for thought travel with Jesus was unnervingly fast. After a bit, her body seemed to settle and she began to take in all that was happening around her. They had come to a hillside, with billowing hills as far as she could see, in every direction, all filled with people. They were singing, laughing, dancing, and worshipping.

Sarah felt a bit overwhelmed at the sheer number of people, which she guessed may be in the millions. She felt the gentle whisper of the Spirit, "Yes indeed, there is a great number, yet every individual on every hillside is precious to us. This is all of the faithful, throughout all of history, who have sought the Name of the Lord. Welcome to the Feast of the Faithful. You are precious, my Little One, Sarah."

"Thank you, my wonderful Counselor. I think I will be OK now that I understand," Sarah thought in response. She looked over at Sweeny, who seemed to be swaying just a bit by the enormity of faithful humanity. Sarah said to her in a giggling chwitter, "I would never have imagined just how many people would be in the number of God's faithful. Wow, this is incredible!"

Sweeny responded, still gathering herself, "It is just a bit overwhelming; I feel like a pipsqueak! What a family, to fellowship with, to get to know, to cherish, to love, and to worship with!"

Jesus hugged them both in a tender moment and then was swallowed up by a gaggle of kids, who, in their exuberance, almost knocked them all down! Sarah and Sweeny eased out of the squealing, giggling kid-bundle and laughed as Jesus joined in their joyful banter. In fact, Jesus began to pick up the kids and throw them like a football and the other kids worked together to catch them, caterwauling all the while. Sarah had never seen the like; she almost fell over laughing. Sweeny was so tickled, she just sat down and gave in to the laughter.

When they both felt quite spent from laughing so long and hard, Sarah and Sweeny drew pensive at the volume of humanity before them. They were both used to visiting with people on a smaller scale and had never experienced such an expansive throng of humanity. There was a beauty and peace that enveloped everything, as far as they could see. Laughter, singing, and the sound of voluminous visiting filled the air. Sarah felt like she wanted to just sit back and soak in the glorious day and yet, she also wanted to jump into the mix and become an active part of the festivities. Sweeny expressed the same sentiment, gave Sarah a huge hug, whispered "See you soon!" and bounded toward a group of friends. Sarah watched with sweet affection as Sweeny was swallowed up in the hugs of family and friends.

Sarah perused the sweetness of humanity, as she pondered what blessings the day held. The sight reminded her of the miracles of Jesus blessing and multiplying small gifts of food to feed and bless thousands. Indeed, there were so much more than thousands gathered before her, but before she had time to even consider just how many people were here, her attention was caught and activity flowed on from there.

From behind her, a long line of revelers danced along the hillside, singing God's praises and gathering even more people in their celebration. Sarah turned quickly, surprised by the sound as they came over the rise in the hill. She smiled broadly and on impulse, caught the hand of the last person on the line and began the dance of the hillside. She caught on easily, as it was a mere variation of the grapevine step she had learned as a child on roller skates. She jumped in on the song too, singing mightily one of her favorite praise songs:

"I know he rescued my soul
His blood has covered my sin
I believe
I believe

My shame His taken away
My pain is healed in his name
I believe
I believe

I'll raise a banner
'Cause my Lord has conquered the grave

My Redeemer Lives
My Redeemer Lives
My Redeemer Lives
My Redeemer Lives

You Lift my burdens
I'll rise with You
I'm dancing on this mountain top
to see your kingdom come!

My Redeemer Lives
My Redeemer Lives."

Sarah danced all over the hills, singing and rejoicing with her brothers and sisters in Christ. More people joined and when they all felt spent, they all laughed at the line of singers/dancers that had grown to more than two miles! Sarah flopped down on the soft grass and breathed in deep of the fresh mountain air. She closed her eyes a moment, just to breathe in of the joy she felt. When she opened them once again, Sarah received another surprise; Paul, and their granddaughter, Pearl were peering down at her, as if they were wondering just how long it would take her to notice them. Sarah's breath caught, and then she laughed at her own jumpiness. She thought, "*Some things never change!*" Then she noticed how very much Pearl had changed from the tiny child she once was; she had grown into a gorgeous young lady.

When Sarah said as much, Pearl was quick to remind her, "Thanks, but you know, after a while, the grace of God overwhelms all the physical. I'm a woman of more than 900 years old – I would suppose the physical changes that used to come with age are obsolete now! I am so thankful for that!" All three of them chuckled at that - Sarah and Paul with a knowing that they were **even older** than Pearl, but with the joy of the Lord ever keeping them youthful.

Paul and Pearl joined Sarah, lounging on the thick grass that blanketed the hillsides. They leisurely caught-up on each other's lives, Paul sharing his joy of exploring music with the full blessing of the Creator of music. Pearl spoke of the great adventures with children and young adults, learning together about life with the Lord. Sarah was fascinated; back and forth they went, each with unique and beautiful stories to tell. Sarah assiduously listened, feeling like a huge sponge - soaking it all in.

One part of Paul's story brought them all to tears of awe and joy. Even he choked-up a bit as he told it, "After working in small groups for quite a while, to get used to the quality of instruments and our new abilities, which Jesus had greatly enhanced, we joined together in a huge concert. It was not too long ago, about 6 months ago, I'd say."

Sarah pondered the timing, for she had somehow missed the concert. After a bit, something clicked into place, like the final piece of a puzzle, "*Ah yes, I was visiting all the groups of people with Sweeny and Jesus.*"

Paul continued his soliloquy, "We joined together along the beach of the Alive Sea (*which was once called the Dead Sea*), thousands of musicians with their instruments. We first grouped into our specific instrument clusters, then made ourselves comfortable in 10 rows deep, spanning about a mile along the shore. Jesus walked out on the lake," Paul interrupted himself, "Oh, and did you know that walking on the water is really comfortable and fun, not like cement or even hard-packed dirt!" Then, he went back to his concert story, "With Jesus leading, we played hymn after hymn, filling up on glorious music and worship. We were thoroughly surprised when even the fish began leaping out of the water, responding with the joy of worship of Jesus. They swam 'round and 'round Jesus and jumped all-together. It was such as profound dance of the fish; it almost looked choreographed!" Sarah and Pearl laughed, as did a few of the people nearby.

One younger fella, whom Sarah recognized from that first class that she had helped Jesus with so many years before, piped up and shared his experience, "Yea, people sat behind you guys and for as far as I could see, along the shore, singing and dancing in the beauty of that concert. When the fish began to dance too, we all fell into a silent awe and just listened and watched as the music and dancing fish honored the Lord Jesus. And Jesus, He just lifted his arms Heavenward and honored the Father. It was powerful and precious, all at the same time!"

"Thank you, George, for adding to the story with your perspective; every person's viewpoint is so very unique. I am truly sorry I missed the concert," Sarah commented. "When Paul began sharing, I was trying to remember why I missed it and realized it was during the time I was visiting with people all over the area who had been in small groups of discontent. It's funny, but with each group, Jesus was there when the people most needed Him. And yet, He was here too. Between the thought travel and the physical, mental, and emotional healing, I am completely unable to keep up with Jesus' total command over every aspect of life – gravity, physics, and even knowing down deep in every heart, to know every person individually and intimately. Wow!"

"I understand how you mean," Pearl responded. "I too, feel quite befuddled by what used to be the natural world, turned upside-down and inside-out with the miraculous truths of living in the Presence of God Himself. It is so much fun to live without pain, to experience all of life as He created it to be, and to live in communion with Jesus, our Father, and His Spirit. It is life-altering, life-affirming, and is filled with a love that we had only an inkling of before Resurrection Morning."

Just as Pearl finished her comment, a groundswell of praise lifted upward from the valleys and hillsides all around them. It was a hymn of praise, of joyous honor to the Lord, for all the beauty, love, and fullness of life in Him. Sarah, Paul, Pearl, and George joined in the throng of voices lifting praises to the Lord:

> "Great is Thy faithfulness, O God my Father
> There is no shadow of turning with Thee
> Thou changest not, Thy compassions, they fail not
> As Thou hast been, Thou forever will be.
>
> Great is Thy faithfulness
> Great is Thy faithfulness
> Morning by morning new mercies I see
> All I have needed Thy hand hath provided
> Great is Thy faithfulness, Lord, unto me."

Sarah mused, as she sang the familiar, cherished hymn, "*I am not even the slightest bit bothered by the old English, Thee's and Thy's; there is an honor brought to the hymn, like the sacredness of the words highlight the depth of meaning in my heart and soul.*" The beauty of thousands of voices uniting in praise stirred her soul and brought tears of joy trickling down her cheeks, as the torrent of emotion spilled over into the physical.

In the moments that followed the treasured anthem, there was such a hush amongst the people that the worship of the wind, trees, flowers, and even the rocks and mountains could be heard. The mountains and rocks released a low rumble, and Sarah thought it sounded like an impending earthquake. But nothing moved that she could see, she just felt the deep reverberation of worshipful movement within the earth itself. Animals had gathered, surrounding humanity on every hillside. Each offered of his own type of worship, some grunting, others running full speed at the far edges of the gathering, or soaring high above in glorious loops and formations. A bunch of the large cats, bears, and smaller furry creatures meandered in and through the myriad groups of humanity, uniquely giving honor to the Creator in voice and gentleness. The trees emitted a flurry of flickering harmonies, as if the leaves held the fullness of worship in their tender grasp. Various shrubberies lifted up pillows of beautiful elegies, each clothed in melodies and punctuated with fun pops, as the fruit of the shrubs exploded in the midst of their worship. The flowers topped off the beauty of nature's worship of the Creator, with unique melodies that enfolded together with all the other resonances in great honor of the Jesus. Angels hovered above the flight of the birds and hummed such high-pitched harmonies that Sarah was surprised she heard them. Their contribution was to enhance the worship coming from nature, not detract from it. Humanity was encircled and infused with the worship and merely rested in awe and silence, as they joined with all of creation in the reverence to the Lord.

Jesus was visibly moved by the enormous manifestation of worship. Sarah loved His response; He so received the love and veneration that He was lifted up into the air. He closed his eyes, outstretched his arms and legs, and leaned back into the joy. He remained there for a long, glorious moment, with no one counting the seconds. Everyone entered into the joy, begin one with each other, one with nature, one with the Creator, and in the very midst of that, one also with Daddy God and the Spirit. There was a unity that held everything in what felt to Sarah to be an eternal moment.

She could hardly pinpoint the details, but all facets of life was superbly highlighted and cherished in that moment. She loved it and saturated herself with it, as if she couldn't get enough. As she pondered life's beauty, its profound unity, and the transforming power within the combination of worship, unity, and the Presence of God, Sarah heard the gentle, gracious whisper of the Spirit, "It is indeed, a moment of eternity. This is just a hint of the life to come, this unity within the Godhead, humanity, animality, angelity, and nature. Enjoy it; embrace its power and fullness. There are always new joys in experiencing life with God."

Sarah whispered, "Thank you, gracious Spirit!" She reposed, relishing in the absolute beauty of this unity. It was like nothing else she had ever felt; it was truly glorious.

After ample time for everyone to relax in the eternal moment had transpired, Jesus raised his hands toward the thousands of people gathered, even the animals flying hither and yon and those running around, and invited everyone to eat of the provision of God in His Feast for the Faithful. Upon hearing the invitation, all of humanity was surprised by huge tables, burgeoning with sumptuous food, came down from Heaven, landing all over the hillsides. People gathered in groups and ate of the great feast God prepared for them. At the same time, huge bowls of the animal's favorite fodder descended and came to rest in the valleys. The animals feasted contentedly, as humanity did the same.

Sarah ate things she had never seen or tasted before. She partook of sandwiches that burst with fanciful flavors and luscious soups that pleased her palate thoroughly. She finished her meal with several deserts, that were so cleverly made that they tasted like Heaven itself. She had returned to the table many times, feasting on the joy of the Lord. She was finally so satiated that she could not eat another bite.

She loved the fun vista of humanity, animality, and angelity. Everyone was content in the fullness of the Lord and His blessings. Hillside upon hillside, and deep in the valleys, and as far as she could see in the air, humanity, animality, and angelity stretched itself forth, glorying in the love of God. Sarah whispered to herself, almost as if savoring the moment, snapping its picture – to cherish, *"The Feast of the Faithful, my Faithful Jesus, and all those who chose to be faithful to Him."*

Jesus stood on a hillside and in a booming voice declared, "To you who are faithful, in your heart, mind, and soul, I will hold you dear. I will protect you and never let you slip from my grasp. We have upon us a short season, in which the father of lies, old Lucifer, will once again attempt to deceive. Stand strong, hold onto this faith, and he will have no power over you. Be strong in the power of God, for We have all power over Satan."

Chapter 21
Attempted Commotion

Sarah gasped, along with all of humanity who were sprawled across the many hills surrounding her. She saw and felt a great belching of the earth. Along with billowing sulfur-smelling smoke, the earth spewed out a singed foul-smelling creature who was unmistakably the leader of all the hideous demons who followed, puked out of the pit for the last season of their attempt to cause commotion among humanity. Satan landed amongst a crowd, plopping down next to a woman who screamed and shuddered, as she scampered quickly away from him. The rest of the bunch retreated in a broad circle to give him plenty of room. They didn't want to even be near the loathsome, pitiful fallen angel. The demons landed splat, sprawling along the hillside just below their miserable leader. They all just shuddered for a while, shaking off the horrible ashes that were ever-present at the edges of their appendages.

Jesus had full control of all of them and they knew it. He specified the parameters of their limited season of partial freedom, "You have only a very short season to do your bidding. Your presence here is not to benefit you, but to test the hearts and minds of humanity. You may not harm anyone; you are bereft of any power over humanity. There is only one provision for your presence among us, to challenge every single person in their choice to follow me. There may be one or two who have not yet made the choice to live a life of grace in my Presence forever. If you are able to roust out any, who within their own hearts are denouncing my grace, power, love, and provision for them, as you have, they have complete freedom to join you. Do your behest quickly, for I will not allow this to linger on."

Sarah shuddered, as the demonic mass huddled together, devising their obnoxious plan to attempt more than what Jesus specified. She could sense the ferocious hatred and putrid plans that emanated from the hoard. At the same moment, she felt the grace-filled assurance from the Spirit that His Presence would overshadow her and care for her through this short time of unrest.

As the hoard jumbled together, rickety in their stance from the burning of their flesh for so long (even though their bodies never charred completely), slurps and burps of misery slipped out of their mouths. Satan tried to lead, but even he felt the loss of power, compared to the powerhouse he used to consider himself to be. He cajoled, belittled, and condemned the demons who gathered around him for direction. His only thought was to attempt a personal attack on every person, at their most vulnerable moment. Their goal was to get humanity, one at a time, to question God, the goodness and grace of Jesus, and if possible, to get them to renounce this Jesus as their "Almighty Savior." Satan spat viciously as he spewed out his plan. "Just try to get every person to let this 'God' idea go and see life could be so nice and easy without any 'God' to worry about." The problem was, (Sarah could sense the discord within his visage) he could not get away from the ultimate Creator, even of his own being. The reality of God was in his face and he hated it with every fiber of his singed soul.

Sarah asked the Spirit, "How am I able to sense what is happening in the hoard of demons? I remember being barely aware of the presence of demons before Resurrection Morning and now, I can almost hear their thoughts!"

The Sprit whispered dearly, "My sweet, you have sought out the truth of the spiritual realms so completely that now, you are sensitive to the movement within that realm. This is a good thing, for it provides for you a wisdom that is of God. Nothing will be able to dissuade you from the truth of

God. This is spiritual maturity; you are blessed to be one who sought out God's truth, both in the physical and spiritual realms."

A flood of grace-laden love engulfed Sarah and she sat back on the hillside and rested in the love of God. She remained so long in His Presence that after a long while, she felt the whooshing of demonic flight above her. As the demons swooshed by, she felt their feelings, more than actually hearing their thoughts, "Don't bother with *her*; she's a goner, not worth our time." She merely laid back, thanking Jesus for His love.

When Sarah sat up once again, a few people had departed to go back to their homes. Sarah decided to meander back and visit on her way, with people she had not had the opportunity to get to know yet. Of the multitudes, there were many faces who were yet unfamiliar. She also wanted to get others' impressions on the events of the day. The highs and lows were quite dramatic and she felt a bit over-loaded and wanted to de-compress a bit.

A little girl came up to her and asked if she could hold her hand and walk with her. Sarah responded, "Sure, I would love to walk with you." She immediately knew her name, Miriam, and told her how pretty she looked.

"Thanks," she replied. "I was named after Moses' sister!" she continued, exclaiming. "I even met her and we are great friends!"

They walked down the hillside, hand in hand, swinging their arms in a playful time together. Sarah said, "How wonderful, to be named after such a gracious woman! Are you doing OK after all this stuff going on today?"

The little one replied vivaciously, with her blond curls bouncing all over, "Oh yes, I'm just fine! My Jesus gave me a very special helper, His Spirit, and I am not afraid of anything or anyone anymore!"

Sarah laughed and agreed, "Yes, He helps me too, anytime I need Him, for any question, or just to be there with me. It sure is delightful, isn't it?"

Miriam smiled sweetly, her whole face reflecting the joy in her heart, then shared, "It sure is! I remember not too long ago, when I didn't know Jesus, I spent a bunch of time confused and angry. He sure has helped me understand things better, see things more clearly, and be a happier person too. He even said I get to live with Him forever, and ever, and ever! I can understand that some, but I know I still have a lot to learn about living in Christ. Is it different from when you were young, Sarah?"

"Oh yes," Sarah responded. "When I was young, I didn't know too much about Jesus, or His Spirit. My family was all twisted up in anger and that came out in hurting each other. Even I joined in, because that was all I knew – hitting, kicking, pulling hair, throwing things at my brothers and sister. I was horrible! When I grew up and learned about Jesus' love, I felt awful about the hurt I had caused. My brothers and sisters also felt rotten about how we had all behaved. We all apologized to each other and forgave each other. Jesus' love changed every one of us and now, we all love each other more than we could have ever imagined. Jesus healed my heart and not only that, my family too! On another topic, How old are you, Miriam?"

"I'm seven, but Jesus said I do not even have to worry about my age, whether young or old! How old are you, Sarah?"

"I'm a bit like you, I don't worry about it very much, but I think I'm somewhere around 1,050 years – give or take a few! If you can imagine, I was a grandma on Resurrection Morning, almost a thousand years ago now! I don't feel old like I did then, but instead, I feel like the days and years are quite meaningless; I do not even focus on them anymore. You seem like a wise little girl, even as young as you are!"

"I think Jesus does that to anyone, no matter what their age!" Miriam quipped. "I have lots of fun, just living in His Presence. And His Spirit said that this wonderful life with Him will go on forever, without any ending of the love of God or His grace."

Sarah affirmed, "Yes, it is very challenging to even think about it, but enjoying every moment and all the blessings that the Lord brings to us in that moment is my focus these days. It is a lesson that He has been teaching me for a while, helping me to let go of expectations, suppositions, and especially, disappointments. I am learning that growing in Christ does not stop; there are new things His Spirit teaches every day, as I remain open to His guidance."

Miriam interjected, "Sarah, I think it is a good thing that you and I became friends. I want to learn more about living in Christ and you are so full of His love and life. It seems to ooze out of you, like boiling taffy, ready to be pulled apart and molded into something so sweet that people cannot get enough!" At this, they both laughed until they could hardly stand up.

The two gals strolled hand in hand, connected not only by gender, but by the very source of life, the love of God. They dipped down the path into a thicket of lush, dense bushes, which were burgeoning with fragrant floras of intense colors. Sarah had never seen such intensity in floral colors and asked the Spirit in a childlike whisper, "How can these be so intense in color?"

His response was audible, for both of them to receive, "It is the power of Jesus' love, for the healing of the Earth, the water and the land, that has led to the depth of color and beauty of not only this plant, but to many others. As the Earth heals, more and more, it reflects the healing and the love it has received. Bless you, my dears, our love surrounds you and upholds you both."

When the Spirit blessed them, Sarah and Miriam were both literally swept off their feet. They both tumbled, giggled, and rolled in the sweet grassy little meadow that opened up amongst the mass of flourishing bushes. They came to rest and leaned back and laughed. Sarah felt like a 7 year-old herself, full of love and mischief - the good mischief like little girls think up - frolicking in fields, climbing mountain trails, jumping into sparkling waterfalls. Oh, she felt full!

Miriam took it all in stride, with the innocent joy a little girl brings to life. It was almost as if the two were one, united in their complete joy.

At last, they rose to continue their short trek back to Jerusalem. They began to sing, linking their arms and their strides,

> "I love to go a-wandering
> Along the mountain track
> And as I go, I love to sing
> My knapsack on my back.
> Val-deri, val-dera
> Val-deri, val-dera
> Ha, ha, ha, ha, ha, ha
> Ha Val-dera
> My knapsack on my back."

Their voices rang true and beautiful, as beautiful as the birds twittering in the trees. Sarah sang alto and little Miriam belted out the soprano melody with gusto; Sarah could tell Miriam really liked to sing and hike! She was having fun with this little one!

The Spirit spoke to Sarah's heart, "You too, are my Little One. You are precious to me. I love the passion you bring to everything you do and say. I cherish the relationship and fellowship we have. Be blessed, my dear Sarah."

Sarah breathed deep as she thoughts flowed from her mind and heart, "*Oh thank you, my Lord. I love everything about living with you; your Presence is ever with me. Your love is more intense and personal than I have ever experienced! How sweet is my life with you!"*

Miriam broke away from Sarah's grasp and ran ahead, skipping lightheartedly, then leaping over a mountain brook. Sarah giggled and sprinted to catch up with the lithe girl. They both ran an all-out race, bounding down the trail that led back to Jerusalem. They were closer to their destination than Sarah realized and abruptly, the trail broadened to a small road and a few houses appeared on either side.

As they finished their relaxing trek and entered the environs of the great city, Miriam coaxed Sarah into visiting her home and her family. It didn't take much effort; Sarah was captivated by the sweet little girl. They skipped the last few blocks to Miriam's abode and her family was just laying out the last of their preparations for a family game night. After giving hugs all around, Miriam introduced her new friend, "Everyone, this is Sarah, my new friend. We had a great time coming back from the mountainside!"

Sarah was quickly engulfed by a bunch of new friends, for in this new life with the Lord, friendship flows as easily as a mountain brook frolicking toward the sea. She joined them in their favorite game, a new take on the Monopoly idea, Christopoly, a fun game of life in this new millennial experience. The conflict that was once the center of such games was gone and in its place, was a lighthearted round of laughter, fun, and comradery.

Sarah played with her new friends for hours and at length, bid them goodbye. She padded her way home, and sank into her favorite lounger with a peaceful sense of joy. She relaxed for a bit, then prepared a bite to eat.

For a while, the days and nights flowed like a lazy river, and Sarah felt like she did when she was just a youngster, laying in a field of flowers on hot summer days. She was happier than those young years, for they had been marred by the daily violence in her home. She remembered dreaming of a life without such pain; now she was living it! She didn't worry about time, but she knew that Satan was busy and was thankful his time was limited. She had heard of a few people who had slinked away to join him. Conversely, many who were questioning about issues of life, sin, and eternity had been brought to salvation, through prayer and gentle encouragement. Her focus remained on Jesus, worship, family, and friends; her life felt enriched, engorged with love, and more full than she could have ever imagined in her youth.

Chapter 22
Crowns of Righteousness

One beautiful spring morning, after a personal time of worship and then a brief rest after the intensity of it, she heard a rapping sound, opened her eyes and realized someone was knocking on her front door. Sarah leaped up, with such energy that she was shocked by the volume of it, coursing through her blood vessels, clear to the very capillaries. She could feel the vitality, as if it were reaching out to her conscious mind, saying to her, "I'm here, ready and willing for every task!" It caught her by surprise, until she remembered her worship time with God. Ah, yes, Sarah breathed in deep and let the air out, whispering, "My Lord and my God."

As she bounded to the door, Sarah merely thought the prayer, *"Make me a blessing to your people, Lord,"* and she intuitively knew it would be done.

Sarah opened the door to a group of young ladies. They sang a vibrant song, an excited invitation,

> "Come and see what God has done, His awesome
> deeds for mankind!"

The ladies opened their hands to enfold Sarah into the group, and as she stepped out, into their midst, they hugged her and they all began together, heading for – Sarah didn't even know! But she knew her Lord; His blessings are real and abundant!

With every block they traversed, more people joined in; Sarah gave Sally a warm embrace when she joined in the throng. They were quickly separated, as the group progressed toward their unrevealed destination. What had begun with just a few people and small steps, grew exponentially to be a great mass of people following the few ladies who knew where to lead. Jesus was preparing something for all believers, to encourage them, but also to bring them to a level of spiritual maturity that they had not known. He gave the task of bringing people in to six ladies; even they didn't have all the details, but they knew the Lord Jesus was preparing for blessing His people more than they had ever known, in all of their years on Earth and then even the years in Heaven.

Sarah recognized the garden they were climbing toward, The Garden of Gethsemane. The beauty of the trees and lush vegetation lifted her right into praise of her Creator. As she climbed, Sarah breathed in deep of the refreshing Mediterranean air; by the second deep breath, she said, "Yah" as she took in air, and "Weh" as she let all the air out. Breathing in again, saying the name of God, Sarah remembered all over again that it was by the power of Jesus that she had the breath of life. She lifted her heart to be receptive and appreciative of whatever Jesus had in mind.

Sarah quelled her curiosity about what Jesus had planned and simply offered to serve Him and His people, if she was needed. The Spirit spoke tenderly directly to her heart and soul, "Thank you, Little One. Yes, you will be a blessing as you trust Jesus to work in you and through you. He awaits your arrival; Sally will join you in assisting Jesus with this very special time of Jesus blessing."

Sarah watched the throng as they arrived, sat down, and worshipped the Lord God. Everyone knew something was imminent; they could feel the blessings, as if they were hanging in the air like miniscule water droplets, waiting for the release of the elation they held. In this garden, Jesus humbled Himself before Father God. Sarah perceived that this was completely different than any other gathering she had experienced while back on Earth. She remembered most gatherings as chockfull with excited discussions of all that God was doing in their midst. This assemblage, conversely, felt powerful in adoration of Jesus. As far as she could see, prayer, singing, and worship abounded. Sarah noticed Sally and stood up to join her, as she made her way to where Jesus stood. He was in communion with Father God and the Spirit, uniting not only with the Godhead, but also with the people of His creation.

As Sarah and Sally approached, they both fell to their knees, overcome by the magnitude of their humanity and the Divine Presence of Jesus, together with Daddy God and the Wonderful, Comforting Spirit. Sarah had never felt as miniscule (yet, so loved) as in the moment when she sensed the all-encompassing Presence of God, Three-in-One, the highest superlative of the expression of love. Sarah allowed herself to be overcome, utterly spent in worship.

At length, Jesus began to wrap up the worship of humanity in a song of thanksgiving, His intense baritone voice covering them in a blanket of love,

> "We rejoice together, in tender fellowship,
> We love each other, forever and ever."

A soft "Amen" drifted among the throng, as Jesus' voice released the refrain. He lifted His arms and shared the vision for this day, "My dear ones, this garden is my favorite place, for it is here that salvation became possible for all of humanity. In this garden, among these trees, I chose to be obedient and humbled myself to the will of my Father God. We are one, bound in unity; nonetheless, the moment of my suffering ripped us apart, and I paid the price for all sin, giving my life for you, that in the power of My Spirit, I could not, nor would not, remain dead. As I experienced resurrection, death was defeated. My joy is this, to live with you forever and ever."

Jesus continued, lifting His voice in delight, for He knew the blessings He was about to deliver, "In this place of humility before our Father God, He has given me a gift, the

Crown of Life." As Jesus spoke, everyone saw coming down from Heaven, a crown that was beyond what words could even describe. It was made of gold, adorned by precious stones, and had written on it, "King of kings & Lord of lords." On the inside, which Sarah could see as it twirled in a circle as it descended to Jesus, it had written, "Jesus, my beloved Son." When it alighted upon His head, Jesus - in His humanity - was blessed even more by the love and honor from His Father. He stepped back, losing his balance for a moment in the weight of such love. He caught Himself amid the "Ah's" of those who had focus on the blessing of the crown and the "OH's!" of those who noticed how it overwhelmed Him.

After receiving His own blessing, Jesus was ready to give His blessing to the people. He lifted His arms and began sharing about what being humble really is, "The honor in humility is the choice to entrust your entire life to the wisdom of God. It is a most difficult choice to set aside one's wishes, and be fully devoted to the leading of the Spirit of God. Each of you has done so, and today, I have a crown of life for each one of you. Each crown is unique; each has the actualities of your individual humility written upon them and has been fashioned to bless you forever. Your faithfulness to God is wrapped up in gold and gems, as precious as you are. Sally and Sarah will be assisting me; as the Spirit leads, please rise and come in a line, similar to those long ago graduation ceremonies, to receive your crown of life."

Sally rose first and Jesus met her with her crown, "Sally, your life is typified as a life of a servant. You have been faithful to show your faith in me by example, by serving rather than being served. As you have humbled yourself before God, We place this crown of life upon your head, forever to be a symbol of our love for you." Sally kneeled and the Lord placed the gorgeous crown on her head. Sarah thought she was going to fall over in the blessing of the

Lord, but she merely lifted up her hand and Jesus steadied her. She rose and walked to a long table which held the crowns, as they descended from Heaven and lay down in flawless order.

Sarah knew that she needed to be next, in order to assist Jesus with the gathering. She felt like her insides were turning to mush; her hands shook as she felt herself falling to her knees. Jesus shared her blessing, "Sarah, you are so precious! Your tender humility before God has blessed not only us, but so many people! You have been willing to reveal even the dark things, in order for our glory to cleanse, heal, and protect your sweet spirit. You have brought many here today, by choosing humility over pride. Here is your crown of life; be blessed for evermore."

When He put the glorious crown upon her head, Sarah felt the blessing of the Triune God washing over her, filling every nook and cranny of her body, soul, and spirit with love. She realized that with every blessing, even more love and glory is given and her capacity to receive is amplified. She felt herself swoon a bit, with the heady weight of such love being poured out upon her. With Jesus' steadying hand, He lifted her into His loving embrace. For a long moment, Sarah attuned herself to this new level of God's love being manifested to her through the spectacular crown upon her head. At length, Sarah felt that she could once again assist with the blessing of others.

The Spirit of God whispered that He was directing people when to rise, to receive their crown of righteousness. They formed lines on either side of Jesus, and Sally and Sarah brought to Jesus the crowns. Sarah had marveled at the sight of the crowns descending from Heaven, in impeccable order for Jesus to bless His family. As each person stepped from the line toward Jesus, He received the crown from one of the gals. He held it for a moment, while He spoke the name of His dear one, and of how their choice to humble themselves before God honored and blessed God and His people. Then, as He lifted the crown, He spoke His blessing and placed the crown upon their head. Sarah and Sally also helped with the momentary blessing overload that happened with some when they received their crown of righteousness.

As hundreds of men, women, and children received their crowns of righteousness, Sarah never tired of helping Jesus. No one got fidgety; fruit and luscious desserts floated from one hand to another in the multitudes. Hours were spent; yet they still watched fervently as each individual was blessed with their own crown of righteousness. Jesus' words of truth and consecration were precious to each and every believer. Sarah pondered, knowing that only the Lord God knew literally everything about each person, their actions and their thoughts. She realized that though she had some knowledge of each person and their life story, only the Triune God has full knowledge and therefore, is fully able to acknowledge their faithfulness to Him.

Sarah also acknowledged that there were some who were not present, choosing instead to live a life of pride and self-purpose. As she briefly prayed for them, The Spirit prompted in her mind, "We too, pray for each one, that their hearts would open to the truth and grace of Jesus' gift of eternal life."

Sarah was blessed over and over as Jesus rendered the crowns of righteousness upon humanity. She witnessed up close, the blessing pronounced upon those whom she loved. When her father, William, walked toward Jesus, she handed the crown fashioned for him to Jesus. Jesus said in a robust voice, "William, you humbled yourself before God in the moment you realized how in your ignorance and pain, you had profoundly hurt those you should have loved. You returned to the faith of your youth, and released your own pain to my tender healing love. When you chose to follow me, letting go of your pride, you remained humble in your heart. This crown is a very special commemoration of your total commitment to a life of peace and love in my power, for I alone have life-transforming power. You are my Vibrant One; your crown has the deep, beautiful stone called Smokey Quartz, symbolizing the vibrancy of your faith. Be blessed, my brother!" Jesus placed the crown of righteousness upon William's head and he fell back onto the floor, sitting down with a "thud." He was taken aback by the joy that filled him so completely; he just sat a moment and smiled up at Jesus and his daughter. He even laughed, sparking a holy laughter that spread outward through the throng of humanity. Sally and Sarah were caught up in the contagious laughter and then, Jesus also caught the tickle and laughed until He was bending over! Finally, when all the laughter subsided, William clambered to his feet, taking care not to topple his precious crown, hugged Sarah tenderly, then shook Jesus' hand, gave a quick hug to Sally, and walked back toward his seat, more blessed than he ever could imagine.

One by one, the faithful came to receive their accolade from Jesus. Sally was so touched when she watched the diminutive dear lady whom she had known as Mother Theresa approach her Lord Jesus. Sally handed Jesus the crown prepared for Theresa. Jesus bent a bit to look deep into her eyes and pronounced, "You, my love Theresa, lived your life as a testament of humility. Your heart was so pure that people were compelled to follow your example of faith in the profound love of God. I give you this very precious crown, for your dedication to show humanity the love of God. The diamonds that adorn this crown will ever express your purity of heart." Jesus placed the crown on her head and she was lifted up, about a foot off the Earth, in an expression of the Holy Spirit agreeing with Jesus of her crown. She received a hug from Jesus and floated to her seat, then gently, the Spirit released His dear one, lowering her to the ground.

Theresa had a new and different expression on her face, from the brokenness that Sarah remembered from so long ago; she no longer held the awareness of all the pain and emotional distress of the poverty she had lived her life to conquer, but a new, joyful peace and a sense of regal blessing. She was, in fact, finally fully aware of the impact of her life. During that brief span of floating back to her place to sit, the Spirit revealed to her all the people who were here because of her, blessed by all of eternity with the Father, Son, and Spirit. Each person she had thusly influenced glowed briefly in a golden ember; there were thousands. As she moved closer to her seat, she could see the ever widening circles of people who were in this great company of believers in Jesus Christ because of her life. It changed her whole perspective of her life; she had only seen the poverty, the dirtiness of life with the poorest of the poor. She had not been aware of how her loving touch taught others to love so compassionately; she had not known how the love she offered had been received. Teresa now realized that because the love she gave was the love of Jesus, it greatly affected people wherever she went. She had offered loving touch, compassionate listening, tender arms ever ready to hug, and loving hands to give whatever resources available to those whose need was so great. Now, she reveled in the knowledge of how God had used her. Her willing and tender heart for Jesus and for people stuck in the hole of poverty had truly brought eternal blessings. She was no longer bent over, as Sarah remembered seeing her in the last years of her life on Earth, years ago. She was now vivacious, young, and absolutely regal in her demeanor; Sarah was enthralled by the beauty she beheld.

Sarah also witnessed her mother, Nancy, coming to stand before Jesus. In a tender gesture, Jesus held her hand, and she bowed to her knees. Jesus said to her, as Sarah handed Nancy's crown to him, "Nancy, you have had a tender, humble, childlike faith in me since you were a little girl.

Your crown exemplifies this life of sweet, innocent faith." He placed the crown, a rainbow of precious stones arching from one side to the other, on her head. Jesus once again spoke over her, "You have received all that everyone desires when they see rainbows, eternal life, blessings untold, a life of fun and joy. Be blessed, my dear Nancy." Jesus lifted her up and hugged her with sweet tenderness. He released her slowly, to help her with the transition of having a portion of His glory upon her head. She embraced her daughter, holding her tight in tender love.

Sarah never tired in her endeavor to assist Jesus; in fact, she felt more invigorated as more and more blessings were given. Sarah and Sally both were blessed in the midst of serving Jesus; both were moved beyond description as they witnessed, up close, Jesus blessing their families and friends. With each crown of righteousness placed on the head of a faithful child of the King, the worship of the people for their God intensified.

For a brief moment, Sarah heard the worship of the angels. She asked the Spirit to reveal to her the spiritual dimension and when He did, she was astounded by the worship of God and the joyous revelry of the angels as they rejoiced over each person receiving their crown. This was the culmination of all their ministry to humanity, the love they carried from the Creator to His people, those precious ones they cherished and blessed. Their praise and worship and raucous rejoicing was so loud that Sarah realized she couldn't hear. She whispered in her mind to the Spirit, "OK, I understand now why it's sometimes nice to not be aware of everything. I would like to focus on each person and assisting Jesus in this precious task." And with that easy request, the angelic merriment tuned out of her awareness once again.

As the sun waned and twilight hastened, beautiful fireflies flitted above the mass of humanity, lighting up the crowned and soon-to-be crowned mass of humanity. The beauty of each crown was profound; each had uniquely formed gleaming stones, shining metal, and precious words of love engraved by the loving hand of God. Words of joy floated among the throng, like beautiful fragrances floating on a breeze. No one tired of listening to Jesus, as He blessed each person. Even those who were new believers found that just being around Jesus, their bodies were changing; they no longer required sleep as they had not so long ago. Long into the night, Jesus continued, blessing copiously. Sarah marveled that she and Sally did not tire, nor did they require food. She remembered preparing feasts back-in-the-day when she was absolutely exhausted, even for several days! She felt so honored to be exactly where she was, so blessed to be a part of Jesus' blessing all of humanity.

The final crown was placed on the head of a dear woman, whose name was Delphina; she had suffered as a persecuted missionary to the dear people of China, many of whom were there directly because of her faith in Jesus Christ. Jesus spoke of her great humility before God and the people of China, tenderly placed her crown on her head and tenderly kissed her cheek, then hugged her fiercely. He was visibly delighted by her love and adoration. Sarah watched, mesmerized, for she was surprised by Jesus' humanity in the very midst of His divinity. He released Delphina and she looked up in His eyes with utter adoration, even deeper and profound than ever before. She turned and walked back toward the throng, the light of Jesus' love illuminating her face with brilliant grace. Jesus turned to Sally and Sarah, held their hands and spoke His love for them, whereupon they both joined the throng.

Jesus lifted his arms amid thunderous applause. Smiling broadly to His people, He acknowledged their worship and lifting His arms toward the Heavens, gave Father God the glory. At long last, the applause waned and Jesus spoke to His brothers and sisters, "You are my dear ones. I love every one of you, with an everlasting love. You are precious, the apple of my eye!" Then He started to sing a blessing over them,

> "Father, my Father, bless your children,
> My brothers and sisters, my co-heirs in your love.
> Give them everlasting victory, ever-increasing love;
> imprint upon their hearts the glory of your Name,
> Yah-Weh, my Yah-Weh."

As Jesus' velvety, baritone voice lifted the blessing, the Father's love descended like a blanket of warmth and tenderness. Every person felt the palpable Presence of the Father as never before. Many were so blessed, they simply laid back and rested in it, completely unaware of anything else in all the universe, reveling in this tender love. Others lifted their eyes and arms toward Heaven, almost like a funnel, for the love gushed right into their arms and face, with the glow of such powerful love radiating from their skin.

Sarah felt completely overcome by waves of the love of God, and yet, she was fascinated and able to observe how the family of God received His love. She quietly asked in her mind of the Spirit, "*Am I able to focus, as I receive the Father's love, because I have been soaking in His love over and over since the rapture?*" The Spirit's affirmation of her rationale was greatly appreciated, since she did not want to be presumptuous about the great love of her Daddy God. Sarah glanced around, watching the reawakening of the people to their surroundings. With every new experience of the love of God, new depth of awareness came into their lives. It seemed as though the love of God was expanding their brains and their hearts to be able to receive a new, profound level of His love, all without changing their outward appearance at all.

Jesus once again lifted His hands and invited the angels to display their joy for all of humanity to behold. When He did so, the throng of believers were instantly aware of the worship of the angels to God. Their unreserved joy, that God has blessed humanity with gorgeous crowns of righteousness, and that Jesus is crowned with the splendor of God's glory radiating from Him, was absolutely breathtaking. A myriad of angels flew in beautiful, synchronous dances above Jesus and His people, singing,

"Glory to God, we worship you!
We honor you and your precious ones!
Glory, Glory, Glory to Father God,
our Holy Benefactor of All Life!
Glory, Glory, Glory to Jesus, our Divine Designer!
Glory, Glory, Glory to the Spirit,
our Exquisite Guide!
Glory and Honor to our God!"

Sarah watched, enthralled by the beauty of the angels' worship. She responded, as did all of humanity, joining in the worship of her Lord God. She let go of herself, allowing only thoughts of praising God for His perfect grace and love. Her arms lifted up, almost with a worship of their own; her eyes closed in her complete release of all of her senses to focus only upon God. Soon, her body had to worship too and she rose to her feet and joined the dance of praise. There was no pain, no focus on the physical, but a total giving of her body, mind, and spirit to honor the God whom she loved. She was enveloped in awe, as she had never been before. It made her sparkle with an effervescent glow. Then and there, without even perceiving what was happening because of her intense worship, Sarah began to fly with the angels, joining with them in worship. She didn't have to think about where to go, or how to do what she was doing; her worship was so complete, God's ever-increasing grace blessed her expression of worship, this dance with the angels.

Many other people joined the sky-dance worship; the beauty was mesmerizing – angelity and humanity full of praise for their Holy God. Jesus was lifted up by the praise of so many. He rose straight up above all the throng of humanity praising on the ground and above the angelity and humanity dancing their praises in the air. He held His arms out and blessed those who honored Him so; in the midst of their active worship, the blessing rolled them all into little bundles of joy. Whether on Earth or in the air, they simply curled up and rolled backward – so strong was the blessing. Their crowns stayed with them, as if they were now a part of each person's visage. Even the angels became large balls of feathers rolling backward, so full of the blessing! When each one stopped rolling, they merely rested in the blessing.

It seemed to Sarah that the day was a beautiful combination of Jesus blessing all of humanity and angelity and they all responded with intense worship. Then, Jesus blessed again, and they responded with higher worship. Over and over, blessing and worship, worship and blessing. After this last blessing, which caught Sarah with so much love in her body that it collapsed and tumbled backward, until with ease, she was back on the ground, she realized she was spent. She whispered her love to the Spirit and whisked to her home by thought travel, not even taking the time to walk home and visit with others along the way.

Once again in the soothingly familiar domicile, Sarah took time to ponder the beauty of all that she had experienced.

Chapter 23
On Into Eternity...

Sarah rested, closing her eyes and allowing her body to relax. She had experienced so much in such a brief time; she felt like she needed to "catch-up" emotionally to the physical and spiritual heights of life with Jesus. Thinking about it, she realized that, whether in Heaven or on Earth, life in the presence of the Lord is profound and deeply fulfilling. She marveled at the blessings of the crowns. She lifted her hand up to feel her own crown, then gingerly raised it off her head and beheld its glory.

As much as Sarah had liked rocks from when she was just a wisp of a girl, hunting agates with her Aunt Erica, her fascination with the gems of her crown grew exponentially. They magnificently reflected the love and power of the Living God. The glorious hues of Heaven and Earth oozed peace, love, tenderness, and compassion. They were of such intensity that they bolstered the gifts that Sarah had already been given. She quietly queried the Spirit, "How is it possible for me to take in all the blessings and all the gifts that you, Lord, are giving to me?"

With a gentle laugh, the Spirit spoke audibly to Sarah, "My sweet Sarah, as we bless you more, you will be strengthened to receive it. Think back to Jabez; he prayed for his territory to increase and that God would bless him. His request exuded faith; he knew if we blessed him, he would also receive the capacity to handle the new and different life. For every blessing we bestow upon you, a greater capability to receive it will also be imparted to you. Our love is never exhausted; our eternal joy is ever blessing you and expanding who you are and further, ever being in relationship with you."

Sarah could only whisper, "Wow, Lord! It's a bit hard for me to put my mind around it, but I sure love it! Thank you, gracious Lord."

The Spirit affectionately ended with, "It is our joy to bless you, Little One."

Sarah placed her crown back on her head, realizing that it more naturally was a part of her than she could ever imagine. It completed her; the Lord created the crown to lift Sarah to a higher level of power and purpose. For a moment, she simply prayed, "Lord, I thank you with all my heart for this beautiful crown. I feel unworthy to receive it and yet, I know in you Jesus, I am made worthy because you are worthy. Your redemption of my soul was completed on the cross and I am made new in your power and might. Oh Lord, I want more to serve you and your people, to bless you and honor you every moment. Lord, show me the next step. Where do you want me to go today; how can I bless you and your family today, Lord? I am yours now and ever more. Glory be to my God!"

The Spirit tenderly wrapped her in His love with His words of affirmation, "My sweet Little One, we receive the honor you give from your whole being. You are so genuine in your adoration; we absolutely love being in this profound relationship with you. Presently, there is no need for your assistance. This will be a momentous day, for today at the Valley of Megiddo, we will end once and for all, the influence of this opposer, Satan."

Scarcely waiting until the final word was spoken, Sarah jumped up with renewed energy, like a panther, ready to spring on the enemy of her soul. She stopped briefly enough to gulp down a delicious glass of fruit smoothie, then bounded out of her cottage to head into the day of victory over everything that sets itself against God.

Sarah felt like running; she felt like there was so much excitement rising up in her body, mind, and spirit that she could barely contain it. As she practically flew down lanes and avenues, she saw humanity flowing out of their homes, joining together to become a throng of enthusiasm and anticipation.

As the burgeoning assemblage turned to the right at the next road, toward the Valley of Megiddo, a tad north of Jerusalem. Sarah mused, *"It was more than just a bit of a walk for the person I used to be, but now, the multi-mile run is like an afternoon jaunt!"*

Sarah relaxed her exuberance a bit, slowing to a walk, and fell into step with people all around her. Everyone had responded jubilantly to the news of the impending end to Satan's miserable influence over humanity. Kids were running and playing; everyone else walked briskly, ran, jogged, and even did backflips. The joy of the Lord intensified every movement, every breath. Soon, there was a solid wall of humanity moving effortlessly toward their destination, talking, giggling, and rejoicing - without a care in the world.

When they arrived at the broad valley, the floral carpet was even thicker and deeper than Sarah had remembered. Some of the flowers were a foot high, with huge blossoms. She estimated the throng of humanity to be perhaps in the millions.

"Indeed," the Spirit whispered in her mind, "Everyone is here, from the whole Earth, and watch, there are yet more to come."

Sarah was able to see in that spiritual realm, as she had learned so long ago. She saw angels gathering the demons, even Satan, into an ugly mass of demonic flesh. Three angels flew around the fluttering mess, fast and furious, so much so that the demons were unable to even focus on them. Once again, the earth opened up, just to the north of the valley. It almost looked like a belching volcano, ready to spew out its muck, but waiting patiently instead, following the will of the Creator.

Jesus rose up to face the demonic hoard once more, for the last time. He pronounced judgment upon them, "You were once beautiful, my creation to hold beauty and grace in your wings. I loved each of you dearly, as I have loved every one of my creation. I gave you the power to choose your way in life, to embrace love and grace, or to choose pride, selfishness, and evil. It was your choice to make and now, you will receive for all time, indeed, all eternity – with no end, the consequences of your choices. You will never again be able to torment these who have chosen a life of love. You will yourselves live in torment."

Upon hearing Jesus' pronouncement, shrieks of horror blasted out of the demonic mess. The angels began to fly even faster, with the effect of rolling the doomed demons in the air, toward the open pit. As they arrived just above the sulfur-hissing pit, the angels stopped and hovered. The demons had been unable to fight against the power of the angels in their super-speed flight, and were completely caught off guard when they stopped. They flopped around in the air and fell, shrieking as they hit the molten lava. The volcano belched a sulfuric spit into the air, which promptly fell back in, just as the earth closed up, seemingly satiated by the new arrivals.

The Spirit whispered to Sarah, who shuddered, "Their bodies will never be burned up; they will always suffer the torment of pain and loss of unity with their Creator. It is irrefutably a serious choice to reject the Lord."

Sarah then watched as angels went about new activities. Some were gathering a few in the huge crowd of humanity who had lived through the millennial reign of Christ on Earth, who had chosen to reject Jesus. Sarah had not known which individuals had chosen in their hearts to reject Christ, but oh, the Lord knew. She did have a hint, as those who rejected Him did not have the beautiful Crowns of Righteousness upon their heads. Still more angels were flying in from far and wide, with those who had rejected

God in their hearts. These were the humanity from all of history, dead in their sins, separated from God by their own choice. Sarah watched in great sadness, as she could see and feel their confusion, remorse, and overwhelming longing to change their eternal destiny. Yet, she also perceived that they were stalwart in their rejection of Jesus, remaining blind to the truth of His grace and love because of their pride. They saw the consequences of their choices looming before them and did not like the look of it.

When all the angels had gathered the rest of humanity from all of Earth history, Sarah looked up and was in complete awe, as a glorious, white Throne descended from Heaven. Jesus rose from the hillside and took His place upon the Throne. A huge book came down from above; it was so huge that Sarah could read the open cover from the underside, "The Lamb's Book of Life."

The angels escorted every person, one at a time, toward the throne. Each person spoke only his name and the book was opened. If his/her name was found, rejoicing amongst the angels and the faithful broke out and the person was embraced and blessed by Jesus and escorted to the gathering place of the eternal. If, however, the individual's name was not found in the Book of Life, an angel drew him/her aside, kindly but forcefully guiding them into a formidable angel-fenced enclosure. The angels closed ranks around the lost, the broken, the rejecters of God.

One by one, all of humanity filed before the Creator, the Sustainer of life, Jesus Christ. He wore royal robes, but still carried in His body the price for the gift of salvation given to humanity, the holes in his hands and feet – left by the crucifixion nails. He was ever without sin, for He is God, above all sin. And yet, he bore in His body the consequence of sin, death, for all of humanity who would receive his gift. Sarah mused, "I'm so thankful that He had power over death; it could not hold Him captive."

As Sarah approached the Throne, she felt the love of Jesus even more than she ever had. She said her name, clear and thankful, for she knew eternity with God was her destiny. Jesus found her name, written there in the Book of Life the moment she had received Him as a little child.

He beckoned her to come. When she did so, Jesus embraced her tenderly, saying to her, "You are my Little One, sweet Sarah, I have loved you from before creation."

Sarah almost swooned with the headiness of the love Jesus bestowed upon her. She felt lightheaded and yet grounded, for this love permeated every cell, giving her mind, body, soul, and spirit supreme health and an infusion of Divine love. She felt like the miracle of Resurrection Morning, the renewal of her body, and the life she had lived for more than a thousand years now, was just the beginning. Keturael escorted her to the gathering place of the faithful, embracing her with lavish affection; Sarah responded, enfolding herself in the beautiful angel's wings.

When the last person had been escorted in the direction of their eternal destiny, everyone watched as once again the Earth opened up to receive its plunder. This time, there was a sulfuric burp so strong, it carried with it a wind. The wind scooped up all of fallen humanity with a whoosh, sucking them right down into its lake of fire and brimstone. It was so fast; people screamed and hollered, but had no time to do anything to stop their momentum toward the pit. With a giant slurping sound, final judgment commenced. Those who chose to reject Jesus would never be in His Presence again.

Sarah released her sadness for those who would live forever without God, for it was their choice to do so and Jesus would not ever force anyone to do anything. "*He is such a gentlemen,*" Sarah reflected, "*His love is so precious, so life-giving. It is hard to even imagine rejecting it. And yet, so many did.*" She breathed deep once again, allowing the love of God fill her and releasing every form of sadness.

She pondered, *"This is the beginning of Eternity! Wow, how can this be? How will life be, living on and on and on...?"*

The Spirit spoke to her questioning soul, "You have entered into the deepest part of what it is to be created in the image of God. We are ever present in the now; every moment is sacred, powerful, and appreciated. Because you were created in our image, you too will now be able to be more fully who you were meant to be, an eternal being, capable of love, creativity, kindness, gentleness, peace, and gentleness. All of the gifts we have placed in you will grow into great fullness. Behold, your new city of life..."

Sarah, and all the faithful of the Lord, stood in awe, as the New Jerusalem came down from Heaven. It's beauty was beyond measure, beyond Sarah's ability to even describe. Her whole being tingled with the excitement, the love, and the joy of embarking upon .... wow, eternity.

Bible References Foundational in Millennial Hope

All things are possible with God | Mark 10:27
A new name given | Revelation 2:17
Christ, the first fruit of the resurrection
| 1Corinthians 15:20,21
Come and see what God has done… | Psalm 66:5
Crowns of righteousness | 2 Timothy 4:8
Garments of the High Priest | Exodus 28
God's Compassions are new every morning
| Lamentations 3:22-24
God's love is beyond understanding | Ephesians 3:16-19
I am fearfully and wonderfully made | Psalm 139:1-16
Jabez' Prayer | 1Chronicles 4:10
Jesus feeds the 5,000 | John 6
Jesus is our High Priest | Hebrews 4:14
Jesus is the perfecter of our faith | Hebrews 12:1-2
Jesus is the Creator | John 1:1-5
Jesus loves us from before creation | Ephesians 1:3-6
Judgement of every person | Revelation 20:11-15
Lamb's Book of Life | Revelation 20:12-15, 21:27
Little Ones | Matthew 18:10
Lord's Prayer | Matthew 6:9-13
Mind governed by the Spirit is life and peace Romans 8:5-6
No eye has seen the things God has prepared for those who love Him | 1 Corinthians 2:9
Heaven and Earth worship God | Psalm 19:1-4
Number of one's days | Psalm 139:16
Prayer of God for us | Romans 8:26

Reigning with Christ for a thousand years   Revelation 20:4
Satan bound for a thousand years   Revelation 20:1-3
Satan let loose for a short season   Revelation 20:7, 8
Satan thrown into lake of fire   Revelation 20:10
Seeking God   Acts 17:27
Speaking to one another with psalms, hymns, and spiritual
songs   Ephesians 5:1
Stones would worship Jesus if the disciples were silenced
                                            Luke 19:39-40
Two or more are gathered in Jesus' Name   Matthew 18:2
We demolish everything that sets itself against God
                                       2 Corinthians 10:5

ABOUT THE AUTHOR

Freda experienced physical and sexual abuse throughout her childhood. She was broken and confused for years. As a young woman, she sought counseling for 12 years. When she began to grow in her Christian faith, she realized the depth of healing in the words of the Bible. She then combined tiny steps of healing with those comforting Scriptures and wrote <u>Flame of Healing: A Daily Journey of Healing from Abuse and Trauma</u>, a devotional with a journal, for in-depth, personal healing. <u>Flame of Healing</u> is helping people in several countries to heal from deep emotional pain from abuse and trauma.

Freda is also an inspirational speaker, addressing personal faith, as well as issues of abuse and trauma with love and compassion. She is foremost a child of God, but also a wife of 41 years, mother of three adult children, and a grandmother of one.

Her second book, <u>Resurrection Hope,</u> is a Christian novel about Heaven, angels, and living in the Presence of God. This novel sparked something very special and has grown to be a series. The second of the series is this book, <u>Millennial Hope</u>. The final novel in the series will be available soon, <u>Eternal Hope</u>, focusing on living eternally in the Presence of the Triune God, the Father, Son, and Spirit.

Freda is becoming a prolific writer; she regularly contributes to a blog at <u>www.goodsamaritanministries.org</u> She is also planning another non-fiction book about spiritual maturity and spiritual warfare experienced through the strength of that maturity.

Freda's website is: <u>www.fredaemmons.com</u>

26173332R00124

Made in the USA
San Bernardino, CA
16 February 2019